A KISS FOR LORD BRASLEIGH

Bella's expression hardened. "You seem to have an answer for everything."

"Yes." He deliberately stroked his gaze over her stiff features. He would prove that life with a respectable husband was preferable to life at the mercy of disreputable males. "Of course, I did not seek you out to discuss my ward. You have been most elusive, my dear."

She instinctively stiffened as his tone dropped in an intimate fashion.

"I have been occupied."

"A pity." He reached out to lightly stroke the curve of her lush lower lip. He felt her tremble. "I particularly wished to see you."

"Why?"

"Many reasons. To tell you that your hair reminds me of the sunrise, your skin the richest cream, and your eyes a midnight sky." His voice became husky as his hand moved to cup the back of her neck. "And to do this . . ."

With gentle determination, he pulled her close; then lowering his head, he captured her lips in a searching kiss. . . .

Books by Debbie Raleigh

Published by Zebra Books

A BRIDE FOR LORD BRASLEIGH

Debbie Raleigh

ZEBRA BOOKS
Kensington Publishing Corp.
http://www.zebrabooks.com

ZEBRA BOOKS are published by

Kensington Publishing Corp.
850 Third Avenue
New York, NY 10022

All Kensington titles, imprints and distributed lines are available at special quantity discounts for bulk purchases for sales promotion, premiums, fund-raising, educational or institutional use.

Special book excerpts or customized printings can also be created to fit specific needs. For details, write or phone the office of the Kensington Special Sales Manager: Kensington Publishing Corp., 850 Third Avenue, New York, NY 10022. Attn. Special Sales Department. Phone: 1-800-221-2647.

First Printing: May, 2001
10 9 8 7 6 5 4 3 2 1

Printed in the United States of America

Prologue

A warm fire dispelled the gloom of the late February weather. Not that many gentlemen throughout the discrete gambling establishment would have noticed the chill air. They were far too intent on the vast stakes exchanging hands. All except the three gentlemen who claimed a distant corner.

With a faint smile, Philip Marrow, Lord Brasleigh, settled more comfortably in his seat as he regarded his two friends. He felt a hint of sadness at the knowledge that they would soon be parted. Simon Townsled, Earl of Challmond, had already stated his intention to travel to Devonshire, while Barth Juston, Earl of Wickton, was honor bound to make an appearance in Kent to announce his proposal.

It seemed like only yesterday the three had been in Europe helping to exile Napoleon. It was a grim affair that had drawn the friends even closer than if they had been true brothers. In truth, it had forged a bond that would never be broken.

Not that it had all been grim, Philip acknowledged. Thankfully, after Napoleon's exile they had traveled to Italy together in escort of the pope. What a delightful change from the stench and horror of war. Glittering parties, luscious women, wonderful food, and such works of art he thought he must have found a bit of heaven.

Of course, there had also been that odd encounter with the gypsies, a tiny voice from the back of his mind reminded him. Strangely enough, that memory seemed more vivid than any other, even those of the war. Not that it should have lingered in his mind. It had not been anything special. One morning, he, along with Wickton and Challmond, had happened upon an old gypsy being attacked by a gang of angry farmers. As true soldiers, they had rushed to her rescue and escorted her back to her people. In reward, she had offered them a blessing. Brushing their foreheads with a perfect red rose, she had muttered: *"A love that is true, a heart that is steady, a wounded soul healed, a spirit made ready. Three women will come, as the seasons will turn, and bring true love to each, before the summer again burns. . . ."*

Ridiculous nonsense, of course. The sort of thing that gypsies offered to the gullible or desperate. But more than once he had awoken in the midst of the night to have the words echoing through his mind.

A faint frown marred his noble features as he pondered the disturbing memory.

As if sensing the brooding in the air, Simon, a tall gentleman with auburn hair and emerald eyes, attempted to rally his friends by lifting his glass in a sudden salute. "What shall we drink to?"

Catching the mood, Barth lifted his own glass, his hazel eyes glittering with a boyish charm. "Lovely ladies."

Philip's smile returned. He was always prepared to toast lovely ladies. And one lovely actress in particular. "The more the merrier."

"So much for the gypsy's blessing." Simon took a large drink of the amber liquid.

"Blessing?" Barth snorted. "Curse is more like it."

Philip nearly choked on his brandy. So, he was not the only one to recall the strange blessing. Somehow, the thought made him even more uneasy than before. Why the devil did those words continue to haunt them? With an effort, he conjured a mocking smile. He was not about to admit that he was unnerved by the absurd encounter. "Ah, but the heat of summer has not yet come."

"You do not believe in such nonsense?" Barth demanded.

Philip rolled his eyes at his friend's accusing tone. Of the three of them, he was without a doubt the most cynical. "True love? Fah."

Simon gave a low chuckle. "I do not know. I loved Fiona this afternoon. Until she threw that vase at my head."

Barth refilled his glass. "Casanova had the right of it. Love is meant to be shared with as many willing beauties as possible."

Philip was in full agreement. He knew that love could be more a burden than a blessing. Far better to enjoy the delights of women who realized that a gentleman was not a stallion to be trained to the lead. With an abrupt motion he rose to his feet. "Let us make a wager."

"A wager?" Simon demanded.

"Let us say . . . a thousand pounds and a red rose to be paid the first day of June by the fool who succumbs to the gypsy's curse."

"A thousand pounds?" Barth growled.

Well aware that his friend was constantly in dun territory, Philip offered him a teasing smile. "Not frightened that you might succumb to the wiles of a mere female, are you Barth?"

"You forget, I am about to be wed. How can a gentleman find true love when he is shackled by necessity?"

"Simon?"

Simon shrugged. "I have no fear."

"Then we shall meet here the first day of June." Philip waited for Simon and Barth to rise to their feet and touch their glass to his own. "To the Casanova Club. Long may it prosper."

One

Although the discrete gambling club was renown for excessive stakes and skilled players, it was with a collective sigh of relief that the elegant crowd watched the two gentlemen call for their carriage and leave the smoky rooms.

It was not that the tall, raven-haired Lord Brasleigh, nor the short, decidedly plump Lord Blackmar were not of the highest ton. Indeed, both were undoubtedly leaders of society. It was not that they were not admired and secretly envied among their peers. But after an entire night of being plucked like the veriest flats, they were all anxious to enjoy less-slanted odds.

Indifferent to the jaundiced glances thrown in their direction, Lord Brasleigh and Lord Blackmar exited the club and stepped into the morning fog. Both shivered after the excessive heat of the club, and briskly moved to the waiting carriage. With the elegant grace of a natural sportsman, Lord Brasleigh vaulted into the high-sprung vehicle, while behind him, Lord Blackmar, affectionately known as Pudding, climbed in with considerable more effort. Within moments the carriage was rattling over the cobblestones toward the more fashionable area of London.

Leaning back in his seat, Pudding, attired in a shockingly brilliant yellow coat, regarded his companion with a sardonic smile. "I do hope you are satisfied, Bras?"

Unlike the more flamboyant Pudding, Philip preferred a more conservative attire. His fitted blue coat was without adornment as it smoothly outlined his muscular form, and the familiar Hessians were polished to a blinding glare. Still, with his elegantly handsome features and brilliant silver eyes, he managed to stand out among the more extravagant dandies.

Now, a small smile of satisfaction curved his sensuous mouth as he thought of the numerous notes tucked into his pocket. "Reasonably satisfied," he acknowledged.

"You managed to fleece every paper scull willing to sit at your table."

"I noticed you were wily enough to pick your own share of pockets."

Pudding heaved a tragic sigh, his blue eyes glinting with an inner humor. "I can claim only trifling winnings. I fear my talents are far inferior to your own."

"Fah." Philip snorted. His companion might enjoy the image of a rather dim-witted buffoon, but it took little time in his company to realize he possessed a cutting intelligence and sardonic wit. "You may save such nonsense for those too innocent or too foolish to realize you are as cunning as a fox."

"Really, old boy." Pudding laughed in protest.

Philip stretched out his legs, allowing his head to rest on the squabs. It was some time since he had last devoted an evening to testing his skills at the card table, and he felt pleasantly weary. "I must say it was a delightful way to spend the evening."

"Surely not more pleasant than being with the charming Miss Ravel?" Pudding demanded in sly tones.

Philip grimaced. He had no doubt the beautiful actress was furious at his refusal to attend the theater the previous evening. Since his return from Italy, he had pursued the delectable dark-haired beauty with unwavering determination. He had been bewitched by her lusty passions and sophistication. But over the past few weeks, her tantalizing flirtations had become more and more demanding. She had clearly presumed that his attentions were an indication that she possessed the right to command his presence.

It was an assumption that Philip was determined to correct with brutal speed. He might have to endure the continual demands of his mother and the annoying disturbances from his troublesome ward, but he would be damned if he would be led by the nose by his mistress.

"Less wearing at any rate," he drawled. "Tell me, Pudding, why is it that females cannot resist attempting to shackle a gentleman to their side?"

Pudding shrugged. "I believe it is in their nature."

"I have noted that you manage to elude any entanglements with the fairer sex," he accused.

"Ah, but that is because my wits are greater than my heart, you see."

"Yes." Philip chuckled. "At least I shall soon be rid of one burdensome female."

"Indeed?"

"I have at last discovered a gentleman—a suitable gentleman—to wed my ward," he announced in pleased tones.

Pudding regarded his satisfied expression with a hint of surprise. "Who is that?"

"Monsieur LeMont."

"Good lord! The tragic refugee that has sent young maidens swooning since his return to London?"

"Yes, indeed." Philip's tone was a hint smug. It had taken some time to find a gentleman of suitable birth who was also in desperate enough straits to accept a settlement in exchange for a bride he had never encountered. But he had been quite pleased by LeMont. He was a shy, rather sensitive young gentleman with a pleasing countenance. Unfortunately, his mother was less commendable. She was a pushy harpy who would no doubt plague the young couple with her managing habits. Still, he would be free of Miss Bella Lowe and her outrageous antics. "The wedding shall take place in June."

Pudding widened his eyes. "Has your ward ever met Monsieur LeMont?"

"No."

"Egad." Pudding gave a disbelieving laugh. "That's doing it a bit brown, don't you think, Bras?"

"It is hardly the first arranged marriage, Pudding," he pointed out with a muffled yawn.

"Perhaps not, but no matter how troublesome she might be, it is rather bad of you to hand her off without so much as consulting her wishes."

"Troublesome? She has bedeviled me since the unfortunate day I became her guardian," he informed Pudding. Although he had never actually met the unruly Miss Lowe—he had assumed care for her while serving in Europe—there was rarely a day that he did not receive a missive from his butler in Bath with some fresh disaster. "In the past two years, I have been forced to hire six different companions in the hope they could mend her hoydenish behavior, only to have them flee in terror."

Pudding appeared remarkably unsympathetic. "Well, Colonel Lowe was a spirited devil, always in the thick of action. It would be odd if his daughter did not possess a bit of his nature."

Easy enough for him to say, Philip thought wryly. Certainly Colonel Lowe had possessed more fiery courage than any other man he had ever encountered. But while such qualities were admirable in a soldier, they were a blessed nuisance in a young maiden.

"I doubt that would be much comfort to poor Regert."

"Regert?"

"My butler in Bath. He has been in charge of my poor ward since I moved her to my estate, and a thankless task it has been, I assure you. When I held Colonel Lowe in my arms and promised to care for his daughter, I had no notion what a hellion she would prove to be."

Pudding gave a laugh. "I must say that I prefer chits with a bit of sauce to them. Nothing more tedious than the milk-and-toast misses that are herded into London every season."

"Then perhaps I should arrange a match with you. From all reports, she is a pretty enough wench if you can ignore her ill-bred behavior."

"Egad, do not even jest about such a dreadful fate." Pudding gave a dramatic shudder.

"Do not fear, Pudding." Philip offered a mocking smile. "Miss Lowe might be a bothersome brat, but not even I would condemn her to marriage with a notorious rake such as yourself." The carriage pulled to a smooth halt in the front of a large town house. With the ease of a man who has done his duty, Philip swept his troublesome ward from his mind. "Ah, we have arrived. I hope you will join me for breakfast."

"When have I ever declined to sample your talented chef's masterpieces? One day I shall lure him away from you."

"Never," Philip swore, waiting for the groom to open the carriage door. Climbing down to the street, he waited for Pudding to pull himself from the carriage, then led him up the steps and into the foyer. They paused to allow the silently efficient butler to take their hats and gloves; then taking an appreciative sniff of the appetizing aromas wafting from the breakfast room, they moved toward the hall. At the same moment, the study door was pulled open to reveal a thin, nearly bald gentleman.

"Good morning, my lord," the secretary murmured in an apologetic tone.

Philip grimaced. John Watson had been handling his personal affairs for years, and only sought his presence when trouble was brewing.

"Good morning, Watson. Did you wish to speak with me?"

"Yes, for a moment, if it is not too much bother."

"I feared as much. I suppose something is amiss?"

The secretary gave a faint cough. "I do have a few matters that I wish to discuss."

Philip lifted a hand to rub the aching muscles of his neck. "Can they not wait?"

"I do not believe so, my lord."

"Gads. Remind me to have you dismissed when I am not so weary," he retorted with wry humor.

Watson gave a faint smile. "Very good, my lord."

"Well, at least allow me to pour myself a brandy. Whenever you approach me with that air of impending gloom, I am certain to be annoyed. Pudding, perhaps you would prefer to go on to breakfast?"

"Actually, I could use a brandy myself." The plump gentleman gave a faint shrug. "Besides, I might be of assistance."

Clapping his friend on the shoulder, Philip led him into the study and crossed to the side table to pour a healthy measure of brandy for both of them. Then, turning, he regarded Watson with a steady gaze. "Now, what has occurred?"

"Your mother sent a message this morning."

Philip raised his brows. "Hardly earth-shattering, Watson. My mother sends a message every morning."

Since his father's death ten years ago, Lady Brasleigh had devoted her considerable energies to keeping her only child tied to her side. There was rarely a day that passed that she did not invent some means of demanding his attention.

It was a burden that Philip bore with as much patience as possible. His mother could not alter her need to be the center of his life. Nor could she comprehend that Philip could possibly wish to devote his time to anyone but herself. Still, there were times when Philip found her smothering needs a source of irritation.

"What does she want on this occasion?"

"It seems that she has heard of a Dr. Benton who she wishes you to contact. She believes he might help relieve the pain in her back."

The words were spoken without emotion, although Watson was as aware as Philip that Lady

Brasleigh's insistence that she was at death's door was no more than emotional blackmail.

"That is all she needs." Philip sighed. "Yet another fool to demand a small ransom for his worthless services."

"Shall I request the doctor to call on Lady Brasleigh?"

Philip's lips twisted. "We shall have no peace until we do." His silver gaze narrowed. "Just be sure he realizes I shall not be bled dry, no matter how devoted my mother may be to maintaining her ill health."

Watson gave a nod of his head. "Of course, my lord."

Philip took a fortifying sip of brandy. Good gads, a gentleman should not have to deal with demanding mothers and charlatan doctors before he had managed to enjoy his breakfast. "What other grim tidings do you have to impart?"

"I have received an imperative message from Regert this morning."

Philip smiled with rueful humor. Poor Regert. He had no doubt been treated with any number of furious tirades when Miss Lowe had received his message that she was to be wed. "Has he prepared Miss Lowe to travel to London?"

The secretary cleared his throat in an ominous manner. "I fear that is not possible."

"Not possible? Absurd. All he need do is pack her bags and load her into the carriage. Bound and gagged if necessary."

"Unfortunately, Miss Lowe has run off."

The brandy glass landed on the table with a loud bang. "Run off?"

"Regert heard her sneaking from your estate late

in the evening. He rose to see her leaving with a small case."

Bloody hell, he silently swore. The woman was without a doubt the most provoking, most ill-behaved wench in all of England. Even miles away she managed to keep his life in constant turmoil. The sooner she was married and off his hands the better. "Why did he not halt her?" he demanded.

"He possessed the presence of mind to realize that she would simply make the attempt to flee again, so he thought it better that he follow her and ensure she was safe before sending for you."

Although it had clearly been the wise choice, it did nothing to relieve Philip's mounting annoyance. "The devil take the troublesome minx. Where is she?"

"In Surrey, my lord."

Philip gave a choked cough. It was not at all what he had expected. "Surrey?"

"It seems she met Lady Stenhold in one of the posting inns. They struck up a friendship, and Lady Stenhold offered to shelter her until she could find a post."

"Aunt Caroline?" Pudding abruptly broke into the conversation, making Philip recall Lady Stenhold was indeed Lord Blackmar's great aunt. "I cannot believe that the old tartar would agree to hide a maiden from her own guardian."

Watson raised his hands in a helpless motion. "From what Regert could determine, it appears that Miss Lowe is posing as a widow in straightened circumstances."

"Egad. Aunt Caroline deceived by a mere chit?" Pudding gave a low whistle. "I have never been capable of slipping anything past the wily bird. Your Miss Lowe must be very clever."

"She is a willful hoyden in dire need of a lesson," Philip corrected through clenched teeth. "Not only has she flaunted my authority, she has opened herself up to God knows what sort of scandalous gossip."

"What shall I do, my lord?"

That was the question, Philip acknowledged in exasperation. He had done everything possible to keep Miss Lowe in comfort. He had opened his vast estate for her home; he had hired companions, music and art teachers, and even ensured that she was given the finest fashions to wear. And in return, she had behaved with a shocking lack of gratitude. Perhaps it was time to prove to Miss Lowe just how harsh life could be without his protection.

"I shall deal with Miss Lowe personally," he informed his secretary. "Send word to Regert that he is to remain in Surrey, but not allow Miss Lowe to realize that he has followed her there."

Watson gave a faint bow. "Very good, my lord."

As the secretary left, Philip moved to pour himself another measure of brandy. His noble countenance was marred by an uncommon bout of annoyance. "This time Miss Lowe has pressed me beyond all measure," he said in dark tones.

A renegade hint of amusement glinted in Pudding's blue eyes. "I must admit she possesses a considerable amount of brass."

"Brass? She is unruly, ill behaved, and entirely ungrateful of the effort I have expended to secure her a suitable husband."

"Egad . . . How beastly inconsiderate of her. One would think that she would be delighted to wed a man she has never encountered, who is solely interested in the blunt you have promised."

The fact that there was more than a grain of

truth in the mocking words did nothing to ease Philip's irritation. He was not without sympathy for the young woman's position, but really, she had disrupted his life once too often.

"I have devoted more than a reasonable amount of time catering to her needs," he argued. "She is nearing three and twenty. Soon she will be on the shelf, and I shall never be rid of her."

"You are rid of her now," Pudding pointed out, a shrewd glint entering his pale eyes. "If she is such a burden, why not simply allow her to remain with Lady Stenhold? It is clearly what she prefers."

The handsome countenance hardened. In truth, the same thought had flitted through his own mind. Perhaps the headstrong young lady would learn a bit of respect if he turned his back on her. But he had instantly dismissed the rather pleasing notion. He had given his word to Colonel Lowe that he would see his daughter properly established, and that was exactly what he intended to do.

"Whether I like the situation or not, she is my responsibility."

"So what will you do? Go to Surrey and haul her back?"

"In time," Philip conceded, his thoughts brooding upon a suitable means of teaching the minx the error of flaunting his authority. He wanted to ensure that she realized the dangers of a maiden on her own. And most of all, he wanted to ensure that she was anxious to wed the worthy Monsieur LeMont. But how? With the swift intelligence that had kept him and his regiment alive on more than one occasion during the war, he shifted through numerous plots and strategies until a slow smile at last curved his lips. "But first I intend to ensure that she never challenges my authority again."

"And how do you intend to accomplish that feat?"

A slow smile curved his full lips. "Quite simply. I shall seduce her."

With great care, Bella Lowe lowered the tray onto the satinwood table. A tiny maiden with curls the shade of minted gold and eyes as dark as a midnight sky, she appeared barely old enough to have escaped the schoolroom. But beneath the angelic appearance was a passionate and impetuous nature.

Perhaps too impetuous, she acknowledged for the hundredth time since fleeing from the estate outside of Bath. What young maiden with the least amount of sense left her only home with a few pounds, half a dozen gowns, and no one to take her in?

Of course, she had been decidedly out of sorts when she had packed her few belongings and fled the estate, she acknowledged. She had only known that she would rather live in the gutters than marry a gentleman she did not love. That was what had sent her scurrying to the local village. From there, she had taken the first coach to London, vaguely intending to seek employment. But much to her horror, she had discovered that traveling in a private carriage with a staff of servants was far different from traveling on her own. At the posting inn, she had left the carriage for a badly needed breath of air, only to be accosted by a group of drunken soldiers.

It was Lady Stenhold who had saved her by inviting her into her private parlor and sharing her dinner. She had then offered to take Bella to Surrey and to help her in her search for a position. Without her kind invitation to travel to Surrey and stay at Mayfield she had no notion what would have become of her.

And it was all Lord Brasleigh's fault.

For goodness' sakes, even the lowest servants were allowed to decide whom they would wed. No matter how difficult it might be for a woman on her own, could it be any worse than being parceled off to a mercenary stranger?

A shudder wracked her slender body. Blast Lord Brasleigh and his interference. She had never wished to have a guardian. Especially not one who was arrogant, coldhearted, and so clearly indifferent to her happiness.

This entire mess was all his fault.

The soft rustle of silk brought a swift end to her brooding, and with a smile Bella turned to watch the elderly dowager with silver hair enter the room.

At the sight of Bella standing beside the tray, Lady Stenhold gave a fond click of her tongue. "Really, Anna, I employ an entire regiment of servants. There is no need for you to wait upon me."

As always, Bella felt a twinge of guilt at the charade she was playing. Although her true name was Annabella, she could not pretend she had not lied when she had introduced herself as Anna Smith. Especially since she had also added that she was a destitute widow searching for a position.

It only made it worse that Lady Stenhold had proven to be so very kind.

"I feel I must do something to repay your generosity."

"Nonsense." Lady Stenhold waved a heavily jeweled hand as she moved to seat herself next to the tray. Attired in a patterned silk gown, she perfectly suited the sweeping crimson-and-gold drawing room. She possessed a regal dignity that Bella could

only envy. "You have more than repaid any kindness by the pleasure of you companionship."

Bella took a seat on the beechwood chair uphol-
stered in a crimson damask silk.. "Have you heard
from any of your acquaintances in regard to their
need for a companion?"

Lady Stenhold poured them each a cup of tea,
then filled a small plate with delicate pastries and
handed it to Bella. "It is far too soon for a response, my dear."

"Yes, I suppose," she reluctantly agreed. How
much more comfortable she would feel once she
was certain she had found a means of supporting
herself, she thought with a sigh. Without control of
her own fortune until she was twenty-five, she was
dependent on earning a salary.

"You are not in a hurry to leave me, I hope?"
Lady Stenhold teased.

"Oh, no. You have been so very good to me."

Lady Stenhold leaned back in her seat to regard
Bella with a pair of piercing green eyes. Not for the
first time, Bella felt a hint of unease beneath the
steady gaze.

"It is the least I can do for a widow on her own.
Such a shame to have lost your husband at your
tender age."

Bella would not blush, she told herself over and
over. "Oh, yes."

"Of course you are not alone. Such a dreadful
war."

"Yes."

Clearly sensing Bella's sudden stiffness, Lady
Stenhold made a graceful retreat.

"I am sorry, my dear. It is obviously a painful
subject for you."

Her mythical dead husband had proven to be

more awkward than painful, and it was with a sense of relief that she was not forced to reply as the door slid open to reveal the small, rather fussy butler.

"Pardon me, my lady."

"Yes, Dunne?" Lady Stenhold demanded.

"You have visitors."

"Indeed?"

"Yes, my lady. Lord Blackmar and Lord Brasleigh."

Lord Brasleigh.

Barely aware she was moving, Bella surged to her feet with a stricken expression.

"Oh, my God."

Two

A brittle silence descended, as Bella sensed Lady Stenhold studying her sudden pallor with a narrowed gaze. Then, realizing that the butler was still hovering in the doorway, the dowager turned to dismiss him. "Send them in, Dunne."

"Very good." With a bow, the servant backed out of the room.

Once alone, the older woman returned her attention to the shaken Bella. "Is something the matter, my dear?"

Bella struggled to rein in the gathering panic. It couldn't be possible. Lord Brasleigh was supposed to be in London. He was busily planning her wedding, the rat. How could he be in Surrey?

Unless he had managed to track her to Mayfield.

No. How could he have tracked her? She had left his estate in the middle of the night, and if any of the servants had heard her hasty flight, they would have stopped her at once. They knew their positions depended upon her remaining at the estate. And even if someone had seen her leave, no one could possibly have known that she had left the posting inn with Lady Stenhold.

So, if Lord Brasleigh did not know she was in Surrey, what was he doing at Mayfield?

At that moment it did not matter, she told herself. All that was important was that she avoid Lord Brasleigh at all cost.

"I must go," she breathed.

"Go? Go where?"

Bella pressed a hand to her racing heart. "To my room."

"But why?"

"I . . . You will wish time alone with your guests," she hastily improvised.

"It is merely my nephew." Lady Stenhold waved a dismissive hand. "He forces himself to make the mandatory visit to Mayfield to ensure his place in my will."

"Lord Brasleigh is your nephew?" Bella stammered, wondering if her luck could truly be that ghastly.

The green eyes narrowed in a speculative manner. "No. Lord Blackmar."

"Oh."

"Do you know Lord Brasleigh?"

"He . . . I . . ."

Too befuddled to simply flee as she should have, Bella found herself trapped as the door opened and two gentlemen entered the room.

The first was a short, rather round gentleman with engaging features and blue eyes. There was an air of lazy amusement in his countenance, although Bella suspected that it hid a swift intelligence. There was also enough family resemblance to Lady Stenhold to convince her that this was Lord Blackmar.

Her gaze shifted to the second gentleman, and her heart came to a halt.

He was tall and dark with hair the color of ebony and features that were utterly perfect. Attired in a dove-gray coat and dark breeches it was evident his large form was sculpted to bone and well-toned muscles. But it was the brilliant silver eyes regarding her with alarming intensity that sent a tremor racing through her body.

There was something deeply unnerving in those eyes. Something that warned her this was not a gentleman to trifle with lightly.

"Aunt Caroline, how perfectly delightful to see you again." With polished charm, Lord Blackmar moved to kiss the offered hand of Lady Stenhold.

"Good God, Richard!" Lady Stenhold raised her quizzing glass to regard the pale yellow coat and breeches. "What a hideous coat. Your tailor should be hung at once."

"I shall attend to it the moment I return," Lord Blackmar promised.

The older woman gave a snort. "What brings you to Mayfield?"

"We found ourselves in Surrey and could not pass by without ensuring you are well."

"You happened to be in Surrey?" A silver brow slowly raised. "How very extraordinary."

"Yes, is it not? May I introduce Lord Brasleigh?"

Frozen with fear, Bella helplessly watched the raven-haired gentleman step forward to offer an elegant bow. It was like a nightmare where she was slowly falling and unable to halt the inevitable crash.

"Lord Brasleigh," Lady Stenhold murmured, carefully studying her unexpected guest. "I knew your father. A remarkably handsome gentleman who broke the hearts of many a maiden. You are very like him."

He smiled with a heart-jolting charm. "Lady Stenhold, a pleasure."

Lady Stenhold gave a sudden laugh. "Oh yes. You are your father's son, all right." Abruptly turning, she waved a hand in Bella's direction. "Anna, come and meet my nephew Lord Blackmar and his friend Lord Brasleigh."

Stepping forward, Bella waited with a sick sense of dread to discover if her fraud was about to be revealed. Lord Blackmar, however, regarded her with nothing more than appreciation as he moved to take her hand and lift it to his lips.

"Well, well," he murmured as he lazily smiled. "Had I known you had acquired such a lovely companion, I would have visited sooner, eh, Bras?"

Firmly cutting between his friend and Bella, Lord Brasleigh took her hand and raised it to his own mouth. Bella felt as if the warm lips were searing her skin.

"Nothing could have kept me away," he said in smoky tones.

With a shiver, Bella snatched her hand free. That silver gaze was tracing her delicate countenance in the most unnerving fashion. "I . . ."

"You are going to quite overwhelm the poor girl," Lady Stenhold thankfully intruded in firm tones. "Come and tell me why you have left London. I suppose you are attempting to outrun your creditors again?"

Both gentlemen politely turned, but much to Bella's dismay, Lord Brasleigh remained close enough that she could feel the heat from his large frame.

A fine shiver raced through her body. Although she had heard all the usual rumors surrounding Lord Brasleigh's fatal appeal, she had presumed it was all a great deal of nonsense. One gentleman was much like another to her mind. But this gentleman . . . Well, she would have to be in her grave not to realize he was indecently attractive.

"Certainly not," Richard denied; then with a smile, he lifted his hands. "Well, only a handful at any rate. It was Bras who insisted on dragging me from my entertainments. He is searching for a suitable residence to set up his ward once he has her wed."

A rather odd expression settled on Lady Stenhold's lined countenance. "Really?"

"Yes," Lord Brasleigh answered. "My man of business has given me a list of several suitable estates, but I was grossly disappointed in the few I have inspected over the past fortnight. I hope to view one or two here in Surrey."

Bella felt her breath catch in her throat. He had been out of London for the past fortnight? He could not even be aware of her disappearance. In his mind, she was meekly traveling to London to be handed over to a stranger.

Perhaps she was not about to be revealed after all.

"Then, of course, you must stay at Mayfield," Lady Stenhold graciously offered.

"How very kind of you," Lord Brasleigh murmured, even as Bella shuddered in dismay.

Lord Brasleigh at Mayfield? No. It was not to be thought of. But Lady Stenhold was already waving her hand in a dismissive motion.

"Nonsense. It will be delightful to have company." There was a short pause as the dowager regarded Lord Brasleigh's dark features. "You have a ward?"

"Yes. A Miss Lowe. I served with her father. Before he died, he requested that I take charge of her."

"Is she not traveling with you?"

Bella trembled, but Lord Brasleigh gave a firm shake of his head.

"No. She is in London choosing her trousseau. I believe all young maidens place considerable importance on being properly clothed before they walk down the aisle."

"She is very fortunate to possess such a generous guardian."

Lord Brasleigh gave a short laugh. "I fear Miss Lowe has never considered herself as fortunate. Indeed, she has done whatever possible to make my position as her guardian untenable. Thankfully, the willful chit will soon be married and no longer my responsibility."

Bella bit her bottom lip as a sudden anger flared through her heart. He expected her to consider herself fortunate? For what? For being exiled to the country without so much as a friend? For having her clothes, her food, her servants chosen for her? For being forced into marriage with a stranger? For making her feel as if she were an unwelcome burden? Just as she had been to her father?

Seemingly unaware of Bella's heated cheeks, Lady Stenhold regarded Lord Brasleigh with a hint of curiosity. "And who is she to wed?"

"Monsieur LeMont."

"A Frenchman?"

"His father was French, although his mother is British. They returned to England several months ago." Lord Brasleigh shrugged. "From all reports, he is a most worthy young gentleman."

"I see."

Bella's color heightened. Worthy gentleman? Oh,

yes, so worthy he was willing to sell himself for a few thousand pounds.

"Enough of your ward," Lord Blackmar said, abruptly intruding into the conversation, his gaze shifting to the silent Bella. "I wish to learn more of the delightful Mrs. Smith. Aunt Caroline said you are here as her companion, but she has said nothing of your husband."

Bella could not halt the revealing blush, but thankfully Lady Stenhold rushed to her aid. "Mrs. Smith is a widow."

"That was thoughtless." Lord Blackmar gave a grimace. "Forgive me."

"It does not matter," Bella muttered.

"Of course it does. We are to be guests together, and I should not like to begin with ill feelings."

"I am not really a guest."

"Of course you are," Lady Stenhold protested.

Lord Blackmar flashed her a charming grin. "There, you see?"

Without warning, Lord Brasleigh turned to regard her in a shockingly frank manner. "Which means that she is not to be monopolized by you, Pudding. I shall demand my own share of her attention."

Dash it all. He was looking at her as if . . . as if . . .

It was all too much for the shaken Bella. She needed time to think. To consider what she was going to do. "I should warn Mrs. Clarke that she will need to prepare your rooms. Excuse me." Without waiting for a response, Bella hurried across the room and out the door. Once in the hall, she pressed a hand to her heart.

Dear lord.

What was she going to do?

***

Sampling the excellent sherry, Philip stretched his glossy boots toward the burning fire. It had been nearly three hours since his arrival at Mayfield, and the first occasion he had been alone with Pudding. Lady Stenhold had excused herself to change for dinner, and Miss Lowe had never returned from her hasty flight. An unknowing glint of anticipation shimmered in the silver eyes.

He had to admit that Miss Lowe had proven to be quite a surprise. He had feared she might give away the game the moment he entered the room. After all, his arrival must have been a decided shock. But she had revealed an admirable spunk. Even though she had obviously been shaken, she had managed to maintain her composure.

Of course, he wryly acknowledged, that had not been the only surprise. He had been unprepared for her luminous beauty. Who the deuce would expect such a hellion to possess curls woven from the finest gold? Or eyes the richest brown velvet? Or delicate features that might have graced an angel? Even her tiny frame was perfectly proportioned.

Pondering her exquisite curves, Philip lifted his head to discover Pudding regarding him from across the room. Hoping his friend could not read his thoughts, he abruptly lifted his glass. "A fine sherry," he complimented.

"Yes. My uncle always kept an enviable cellar." Pudding paused, then abruptly narrowed his gaze. "What do you think of Miss Lowe? Will she flee?" he demanded.

Philip shrugged without concern. "I have ensured that my groom will keep a close eye on her, as well as two servants who I have ordered to stay at the local inn. If she flees, I will be close behind. But it is my guess that she will attempt to bluff her way through. After all, she cannot have much money and has few places to hide."

A slow smile curved Pudding's lips. "She is a remarkably pretty wench."

"Oh, yes, quite angelic," Philip acknowledged, feeling the instinctive quickening of his blood. "A pity she possesses the temperament of a shrew."

"That is hardly fair," Pudding drawled. "You know nothing of her."

"I know that she has managed to terrify experienced companions, bully an entire household of servants, and flaunt my desires at every turn."

"I found her quite charming."

Philip narrowed his gaze. He might have been caught off guard by Bella Lowe, but that made her no less a bundle of trouble. "It is not too late for me to change bridegrooms."

"Not me." Pudding chuckled as he settled himself on the window seat. "I am quite content with my life as it is. Besides, I should make a ghastly husband."

"Yes," Philip agreed.

"So how do you plan to begin your campaign?"

Philip sipped the sherry, carefully considering how he intended to proceed. He had every intention of frightening Miss Lowe into marriage. Beginning with a sharp lesson in what a young maiden could expect without the protection of a husband or guardian.

"I shall have to be careful not to pounce too swiftly. I do not wish her to become suspicious."

"Did you ever consider the notion that she might not repel your advances?"

Philip felt an absurd twinge of annoyance at the

question. Good lord, whatever was Pudding thinking? This was his ward, not some common actress. "Whatever her numerous faults, she has been raised as a lady."

"Even ladies do foolish things when they imagine themselves in love," Pudding murmured with a knowing expression.

Philip gave a shake of his head. "I shall make it painfully obvious that my intentions are thoroughly dishonorable and without pretense of romantic nonsense."

The blue eyes twinkled. "Not too dishonorable, I hope?"

"Very amusing," Philip said in dry tones.

"She is very beautiful."

"She is also my ward, in the event that you have forgotten," he retorted, refusing to consider the notion that he had not thought of her as his ward when he had first laid eyes upon her. At that moment, he had only thought that she was perhaps the loveliest maiden he had ever seen. "I will simply ensure that she is aware of the dangers of being a young lady on her own. Soon enough she will be anxious to wed Monsieur LeMont."

"We shall see . . ." Pudding murmured; then glancing out the window that offered a view of the terraced garden, he suddenly leaned forward. "Ah."

"What is it?"

"I believe I see your lovely ward making a dash for the woods."

With a smooth motion, Philip was on his feet and crossing to the window. Glancing over at the gardens, he caught sight of the slender maiden scurrying down a path that led directly to the nearby woods. "She certainly appears to be in a hurry. Perhaps I should join her and discover what has her so troubled."

"Yes."

Setting aside his glass, Philip offered his companion a mocking bow before leaving the room and making his way to a side door that led to the garden. Stepping into the spring sunshine, he used his long strides to skirt the ornamental pond and moved toward the stream that ran in the direction of the woods. He was clever enough not to directly follow Bella. He would come from the opposite direction, as if he had been out examining the grounds.

Entering the woods, he caught sight of a tall man lazily holding a fishing pole over the stream. It was one of the servants that he had sent to the local inn, and with a brief nod, he hurried past him. Miss Lowe would find it a difficult task to flee his grasp again, he acknowledged.

It took several moments, but at last he could hear the soft sound of footsteps, and with perfect timing he stepped on the path in front of the startled Bella Lowe.

Not surprisingly, she took a hasty step backward, her velvet eyes wide with dismay. He was clearly the last person she had expected, or wanted to encounter.

"Well met, Mrs. Smith," he murmured with his most charming smile.

"Lord Brasleigh."

"This is an unexpected pleasure. I thought you were busily plotting with Mrs. Clarke for care of our rooms."

Her delicate bosom heaved as she struggled between fleeing and putting on a brave face. Then, with a spirit he couldn't help but admire, she squared her shoulders.

"I wished a breath of air."

"Then we are of a like mind." He smoothly stepped closer. "I also dislike being inside when there is such promising weather. And of course, a short stroll gives me the excuse to investigate the local rivers in the hope of finding a bit of sport with the fish."

"Then, I will not keep you from your investigations."

"Nonsense." He reached out to lightly clasp her elbow. She shivered beneath his touch. "I may enjoy fishing, but I far prefer being in the company of a lovely lady."

A flare of panic rippled over her countenance at the deliberate manner with which he studied her lush mouth. "I really should return to Lady Stenhold."

"I believe she is resting," he countered. "So you see, there is no hurry."

"Still . . . I . . ." Her words abruptly halted as he stepped far closer than was proper.

"I have not offended you, have I, Mrs. Smith?"

"It is not that," she stammered.

"You seem nervous."

A tiny tongue peeked out to wet those rose-kissed lips.

"Not at all."

"Then you will join me in my stroll?"

He watched her through narrowed lids as she smothered the longing to bolt.

"I . . . very well."

Taking her arm, he wrapped it firmly through his own and led her through the dappled shadows of the lane. In the air, he could smell the faint scent of lavender from her golden curls. A gentleman could easily be distracted by such a tantalizing aroma, and with an effort he schooled his wayward fancies. "Tell me, Mrs. Smith, how long have you been a widow?"

Her gaze remained stoically trained on the path ahead. "Just over a year, my lord."

"You must have been very young when you wed."

"I am older than I appear."

His gaze stroked over her profile. That was true enough. Although he knew her to be almost three and twenty, she appeared as young and untouched as any debutante. "Was your husband a military man?"

"Yes."

Her tone was hardly encouraging. Of course, Philip could not resist. "Smith." He rolled the name slowly off his lips. "I believe I knew an Edward Smith. He served with Wellington. And a David Smith who was stationed in Austria. Are they relations?"

"No."

"What of Robert Smith?"

"No."

He swallowed a chuckle. "Well, I suppose Smith is rather a common name."

"Yes. Yes, it is."

Obviously uneasy at his probing, Bella attempted to hurry their steps. Her efforts merely succeeded in causing her to stumble over a rock in the road, and she lunged to the side. Philip managed to keep her upright, although she brushed into an overhanging branch.

With a wicked smile, Philip pulled her to face him.

"Wait," he murmured as he reached a hand to stroke her satin hair.

With a tiny gasp, she leaned away from him. "My lord, what are you doing?"

"You have a leaf in your hair," he explained, plucking the offending leaf from her curls. Then, with gentle care, he brushed his fingers over her wide brow and down her cheek. "How very beautiful you are, Mrs. Smith. I believe I could gaze upon such beauty forever."

Three

If asked, Bella Lowe would have sworn that nothing could be more shocking than the arrival of Lord Brasleigh at Mayfield. After all, how monstrous did her luck have to be to bring him to Surrey just when she'd hoped she had escaped his unwelcome interference?

Now she realized the shocks were just beginning. There was no mistaking that persuasive smile, nor the intimate stroke of his fingers. Only a looby would not realize he was flirting with her.

Good heavens, hadn't she swiftly learned since her impetuous flight that gentlemen considered such women open to their advances? She had been battling off a drunken soldier when Lady Stenhold had rescued her at the inn. Still, she had not expected such behavior from her own guardian. Even if he had no notion she was his ward.

Now she shivered as those fingers moved to the curve of her neck. Her fear was causing all sorts of disturbing tremors to race through her body. "Please, my lord," she at last choked, forcing herself to take a step backward.

Undaunted, he followed until he was once again

standing far too close. "What? Am I not allowed to tell you that I find you extraordinarily lovely?"

Bella, of course, had heard all the scandalous gossip surrounding her guardian. It was said that he broke hearts by simply strolling through the room. She had also heard that he possessed a lovely mistress. Clearly that did not halt him from attempting to seduce whatever lady happened to be available.

The . . . toad.

The thought helped to ease her rising panic. She would not allow him to frighten her into a hasty flight. Not when she had found a safe haven. Nor would she confess the truth. She was quite capable of fending off a lecherous rake for the few days he would be at Mayfield, wasn't she? And someday she would take great delight in tossing his reprehensible behavior back in his handsome countenance.

"I would prefer that you did not," she retorted in admirably firm tones.

"Why?"

"It is not proper."

He gave a low chuckle. "And you always do what is proper?"

Bella refused to blush. Whatever she had done was only out of desperation. And any blame could be directly laid at this man's door. "Whenever possible."

His gaze stroked over her pale features. "I cannot be the first gentleman to be attracted to you."

"You do not even know me."

"I know that you made my blood stir the first moment I laid eyes upon you." He shrugged. "What else matters?"

Her breath caught. He was nothing if not blunt. And insulting. "Really, my lord, you are impertinent."

"No," he protested softly. "I am honest."

"Well, I do not care for your particular brand of honesty."

He appeared thoroughly unrepentant. "Why? Because I know what I want?"

With an effort, Bella resisted the urge to stomp on one of his glossy boots. The realization that Lord Brasleigh was an out-and-out bounder did not lessen her risk of discovery. "Must I remind you that I am a guest of Lady Stenhold?"

Her cool reprimand was greeted with a widening of his wicked grin. "Not at all. I have been thanking heaven above since I discovered you standing in the drawing room. I had resigned myself to a tedious visit with Lady Stenhold; you have ensured that my visit will be anything but tedious."

He was worse than a toad, she told herself. He was a . . . common lecher. Had she not made it painfully clear she possessed no interest in a flirtation? Was he so arrogant he could not believe that a woman could resist his advances? Or perhaps no woman had ever told him no, she seethed. Goodness knew that he was wretchedly handsome and of a social position to cause most women to overlook his overtly flawed character.

Obviously she would have to be even more blunt. "Sir, I must inform you that if you insist on treating me with disrespect I will have to leave Mayfield."

The silver eyes narrowed at her sharp tone, but his smile never faltered. "Ah, you feel I am being too impetuous. Very well. As an angler, I have learned the art of patience. I will lure my catch with greater care, if you prefer. Until later, my dear."

With a swift movement, he grasped her hand and lifted it to his lips.

Bella instinctively pulled her fingers free, but not

before a startling heat flooded down her arm. She opened her mouth to inform the impossible man that he could possess the patience of Job and it would do no good. But with a brief bow, he was turning and disappearing into the woods as abruptly as he had arrived.

A harsh breath rushed past her lips. The fear that had knotted her stomach and made her head ache had receded during the shocking encounter. Now she felt a seething indignation.

For three hours she had struggled to convince herself that she could endure Lord Brasleigh's visit by remaining meekly in the background and never drawing attention to herself. Unfortunately, she realized the boorish gentleman wasn't about to allow her to remain in the background. He had determined she would add a bit of sport to his dull visit, and he wasn't about to consider her own feelings in the matter.

So what did she do now?

She was not about to return to the estate near Bath. Not when the threat of being bartered to a stranger still hung over her head like a guillotine. And she had learned her lesson in foolishly rushing into the world with no destination and little money.

Blast Lord Brasleigh.

It had been bad enough to be raised without a mother and with a father who was rarely in the country. She had been shuttled from schools to various families that had been paid to take her in. She had never possessed a home of her own or a family. There had never been anyone to care about her unless they were being paid to make the pretense. But still, she had always been able to cherish the dream that she would one day fall in love and create a home and family of her own. It was what had kept her spirits intact.

Lord Brasleigh had tried to steal even that.

Blast. Blast. Blast.

Well, she would not allow him to frighten her into another mistake. She would remain at Mayfield even if she had to fight off Lord Brasleigh night and day.

Somehow she would find a home of her own.

Turning on her heel, Bella determinedly made her way back to the sprawling manor. For once, she was not charmed by the rambling stone structure or Gothic windows. Her thoughts instead brooded on the evil fate that had forced Lord Brasleigh into her life.

Entering through a side door, Bella was on the point of climbing the stairs to her chambers when Lady Stenhold appeared in the hallway. "Oh, Anna, there you are. I have been searching for you."

Suppressing the urge to simply continue up the stairs and lock herself in privacy, Bella instead forced a stiff smile to her pale countenance. "I am sorry. I went for a walk."

"Do not apologize." The older lady advanced, her sharp eyes searching Bella's tense expression. "You are a guest, and are free to come and go as you please."

As always, Bella felt a tiny pang at Lady Stenhold's open kindness. She could only wish there were no need for deception. How wonderful it would be if she were truly just a guest. "Thank you."

"You seem troubled, my dear. Is something the matter?"

Lord Brasleigh was the bloody matter. "It is nothing," she forced herself to say.

Lady Stenhold was far too shrewd to be so easily misled. "You mustn't fret over our unexpected guests. As soon as Lord Brasleigh has inspected his estates, I am certain they will swiftly be on their way back to London."

"I hope you are right," Bella breathed.

Lady Stenhold smiled in an encouraging manner. "Of course I am. Richard is notoriously attached to the entertainment of town. He will not linger long."

Bella could only pray she was right. "I should change for dinner."

"Do not worry, Anna. Everything will be fine."

Simple enough for her to say, Bella acknowledged as she slowly turned to climb the stairs. She was not the one on the run from her guardian, using a false name, and being pursued by a common rake.

Bella did not think anything would be fine for a long time to come.

Although not an excessively temperamental servant, Lord Brasleigh's valet could reveal his disappointment in his young master without uttering a word. Waiting with wounded calm as Philip strolled into his chambers a mere half hour before he was due downstairs for dinner, Ludwin set about his tasks with a decided air of martyrdom.

Unfortunately for the servant, Philip was far too intent on his own thoughts to fully appreciate the masterful performance. Instead, he reviewed his day with a sense of satisfaction.

He was quite certain that he had made a promising beginning in taming his shrew of a ward. There had been no mistaking her outraged panic at his heavy-handed flirtation. Or the hint of fear deep in those dark eyes.

Of course, he had taken care not to force her into flight. He was willing to devote a few days to teaching the chit a lesson. And if he were perfectly honest, he could not deny that his initial anger at being forced into such extreme measures had been eased at the unexpected pleasure in teasing the minx. There was something rather amusing in watching the flash of those dark eyes and revealing color that bloomed beneath her angelic countenance.

With a sense of anticipation, he waited for his grim-faced valet to smooth the indigo-blue coat over his broad shoulders and give his raven hair a last brush. Then, collecting the small box he had acquired in the village that afternoon, he left his chambers to walk the short distance to Bella's rooms.

A part of him acknowledged that he was behaving rather badly. He had, after all, already given her a sample of what could occur to a lovely maiden on her own. But another part of him urged him to continue the charade until she came to her senses. What if she were to bolt again, and this time he could not find her? There were any number of gentlemen willing to do far worse than he had.

The mere thought of the tiny maiden in the clutches of some debauched lecher was enough to make his heart clench in a most peculiar fashion. It also made him more determined than ever to make Bella Lowe realize how foolish she was behaving.

With his resolve once more intact, Philip moved to the door and sharply rapped on the smooth wood. He paused for only a moment; then as he heard her call to enter, he pushed the open door and stepped inside.

At his entrance, she was seated at a window seat, gazing into the growing dusk. For a moment he was allowed to appreciate the delicate beauty of her profile and the slender frame shown to advantage in the simple lilac gown.

Had he been of a fanciful nature, he might have thought he had never seen such a lovely sight—the shimmer of fire in her golden hair, the curve of her shoulders, the proud tilt of her head. But thankfully, he was far too immune to the wiles of women to be swayed by mere beauty.

Collecting his wayward thoughts, Philip was prepared as Bella slowly turned toward the door. Clearly expecting a servant, her eyes widened at the sight of his large form. With awkward motions, she scrambled to her feet and regarded him with angry dismay. "My lord."

Philip raised a restraining hand as he strolled forward. "Yes, I know I should not be here, so there is no need to utter that reprimand trembling on your lips. I merely wished to bring you this."

She eyed the proffered box as if she feared it might contain the plague. "I have no desire for presents, my lord."

"It is a mere trifling." He moved to press the box into her unwilling hand. "A pretty fan that I purchased in the village."

She futilely attempted to hand the box back to him. "No, thank you."

"You would not be so unkind as to refuse my gift?" he protested.

Her tiny nose flared as she struggled to censure the words of condemnation that rose to her lips. She clearly wished him in Hades. "My lord, perhaps

I did not make myself clear. I have no interest in a . . . a . . ."

"Flirtation?" he helpfully supplied.

"Precisely."

"Oh, you made yourself clear, and I must admit that at first I was disappointed." He ran a deliberate gaze over her slender form. "But now I have realized your way is far preferable."

Her arms instinctively clasped about her waist as if to ward off his thorough survey. "My way?"

"Victory is always much sweeter when one must struggle to achieve it." He smiled with devilish amusement. "And I have a feeling that our struggle is bound to be quite delicious."

"I am not playing games, my lord," she said through gritted teeth. "I wish you to leave me in peace."

He chuckled. "Yes, of course."

"I am serious, my lord."

His smile abruptly faded as he reached out a hand to lightly brush the frantic pulse at the base of her neck. "So am I, Mrs. Smith. And I warn you that I always get what I want."

She jerked from his touch as if she had been burned, and with a sardonic bow, Philip turned to stroll back out of the room. He had barely closed the door when the sound of a loud crash echoed through the thick wood.

Philip tilted back his head to laugh with rich amusement. So the hellcat was not as in control of her emotions as she tried to pretend. Surely it could not be long before she accepted that marriage was preferable to such advances?

Across the corridor, another door opened to reveal Pudding attired in his familiar brilliant yellow coat. The outrageous attire had become as much a part of him as his sharp wit.

Catching sight of Philip, the gentleman moved to join him. "Is something amusing?" he demanded at Philip's wide smile.

"Mrs. Smith," Philip explained at the same moment another crash splintered the air.

"It does not sound as if she is similarly amused," Pudding pointed out the obvious.

"No, but she is realizing how vulnerable she has made herself."

"Will you tell her the truth?"

Philip gave a shake of his head. "Not until I am convinced she will wed Monsieur LeMont without causing me further annoyance. Come, I am starving."

Two hours later, Philip sat back with a small smile. Although he was never one to overindulge, he had been hard-pressed to resist the delectable courses that had been laid before him. He might pride himself on possessing the finest chef in England, but he very much feared that Lady Stenhold's artist in the kitchen held the upper hand.

Perhaps he would make an effort to gain the acquaintance of the cook before leaving Mayfield. His hunting lodge could certainly benefit from such talent.

Allowing a hovering servant to replenish his wine, Philip raised it toward his hostess. "My compliments on a delightful meal, Lady Stenhold."

"Thank you." Lady Stenhold gave a gracious nod of her silver head. "Tell me, Lord Brasleigh, which estates are you viewing?"

Thankfully, Philip had requested his secretary discover a few suitable locations before leaving for Surrey. "There is a small estate north of Egham and an old vicarage just beyond Marchwood that possesses a few acres."

"Does your ward prefer Surrey, my lord?" Lady Stenhold demanded.

Philip gave a vague shrug. "I haven't the faintest notion."

He heard the soft rasp as Bella drew in a sharp breath. She had been all but silent throughout the meal, but his negligent comment had obviously struck a nerve.

"You do not appear overly concerned with her happiness," she charged in low tones.

He slowly turned to meet her glittering gaze. "On the contrary. I have provided her a home, an education, a generous supply of clothing, and now a suitable husband complete with a new estate. I have clearly done little else but consider her happiness."

She failed to reveal the faintest hint of apology. "Did you inquire if she wishes a husband and a new estate?"

"You appear remarkably concerned for my ward, Mrs. Smith."

Her gaze abruptly dropped to her barely touched plate. "I merely sympathize with a young lady who has no control over her future."

Philip leaned forward, for the moment forgetting the interested onlookers. "What control do any of us have, Mrs. Smith? We are all bound by duty and obligations."

She lifted her gaze at his challenge. "You are free to choose what will become of your life."

"Am I?" His lips unconsciously twisted. "Do I not have responsibilities to my estate? To the servants

who depend upon me for their livelihood? To my
mother and, of course, to my ward?"

"That is hardly the same."

"How is it different?"

"You are not being forced to wed."

"I shall eventually have to wed and produce an
heir."

Her lips thinned with exasperation at his thoroughly logical arguments. "But to a bride of your
choice."

He gave a short laugh at the thought of the debutantes that had been paraded before him. "From a
very limited selections of eligible maidens."

Clearly as stubborn as she was impetuous, two
highly undesirable traits, the minx regarded him
with a defiant expression. "You at least have the
opportunity to search for love."

"Love?" He raised his brows in a faintly mocking
fashion. "And what do you consider love to be, Mrs.
Smith?"

A startling hint of vulnerability entered her dark
eyes. "Respect. Common interest. The enjoyment of
each other's company."

A tiny pang of remorse briefly tugged at Philip's
heart before he was sternly smothering the unwelcome sensation. Did she hope to discover love by
lying and pretending to be someone else? She was
far more likely to be attacked and left a broken
woman. Far better to have a stable home with a
gentleman who would treat her with kindness.

With a deliberate effort, he allowed his gaze to
drift to the modest cut of her gown. "And passion?" he murmured.

She colored at his provocative tone, but her gaze
never wavered. "Of course."

"Was that the love you enjoyed with your husband?"

He did not miss the quiver that ran through her slender body.

"I was speaking in general, my lord."

An awkward silence fell at her low words; then taking command of the situation, Lady Stenhold rose to her feet. "Perhaps we should leave the gentlemen to their port. Come along, Anna."

Four

In the interest of dutifully preserving the charade, Philip rode off from Mayfield three days later with Pudding in tow. Their destination was formally announced to be the estate north of Egham that he was to view for his ward, but instead they devoted a pleasant day at a rousing boxing match held several miles away.

Philip managed to come away several pounds richer, although his day had been somewhat marred by the realization that Miss Bella Lowe had never been far from his thoughts.

Perhaps because she was nothing like he had expected. She was bold, but not brass or vulgar, and while she was clearly stubborn beyond reason, there was a decided hint of vulnerability that had caught him off guard. And perhaps most startling of all, was the knowledge that he was thoroughly enjoying his little game.

He enjoyed bantering against her swift wit and watching that delightful blush stain her cheeks when he uttered a provocative remark. He enjoyed the feel of her satin skin beneath his fingers. And he enjoyed her constant struggle to sheath her claws and pretend to be a demur companion when she wanted nothing more than to slap his face.

Of course, over the past few days, she had gone to excessive lengths to avoid his companionship. She seemed to have discovered the need for an endless stream of visits to the poor, to the vicarage, to a bedridden widow, and the local school. When she was at Mayfield, she never strayed from the side of Lady Stenhold—which only sparked his purely male determination to outwit her at her own game.

With that thought in mind, he forced Pudding to leave his entertainment and return to Mayfield earlier than anyone could have suspected. Despite Pudding's dramatic protests that he would expire if he were forced to leave before the final bout, Philip's efforts were rewarded when he entered the estate and discovered that Mrs. Smith was currently in the hothouse choosing some flowers for Lady Stenhold.

With a hurried step, he made his way through the vast house to the east wing that was attached to the hothouse. He did not bother to consider why a small smile was curving his lips or why his step was so brisk.

Instead, he readied himself for his role as the determined seducer. Entering the hothouse, he swiftly spotted Bella standing beside a bank of daffodils. Just for a moment he came to an abrupt halt, captured by the sight of her almost unearthly beauty. With the sunlight shimmering off her golden hair and the simple amber gown revealing her slender form, she might have been the goddess of spring come to life.

His gaze lingered on the sweet curve of her mouth, the line of her jaw; then as it slowly lowered to the tender curve of her bosom, he abruptly came to his senses.

Good lord, this was no young maiden to be admired. It was his ward. A five-foot bundle of trouble that had caused him nothing but headache since the unfortunate day she had become his responsibility.

Schooling his wayward thoughts, he determinedly stepped forward. "What a beautiful vision," he murmured.

At the sound of his voice, she turned sharply, her peaceful expression changing to one of utter annoyance. "My lord." She struggled to keep her voice civil. "I did not realize you had returned."

His lips twitched as he strolled forward. He had no doubt that if she had suspected he was about to return, she would have scuttled far away. "The estate proved to be most unsuitable, so there was no need to linger. Besides, I was in a hurry to return to Mayfield."

Trapped among the flowers by his broad form, she had no choice but to brave out the unexpected confrontation. "It seems you shall have to search elsewhere for your ward's new estate."

Philip shrugged, not about to be dismissed so easily. "I still have the vicarage to view."

Her lips tightened. "I am surprised you are going to such effort. Surely an agent could locate a suitable residence?"

"I am not a thorough ogre, my dear," he purred. "I wish to ensure that any estate I purchase will provide a comfortable home for Miss Lowe."

Not surprisingly, she appeared far from impressed by his concern. "How thoughtful."

"I do try."

Her grip on the flower basket was so tight her knuckles were white. "And you expect her to appreciate your efforts?"

His grimace was genuine. "I would have to be a witless fool to expect appreciation from my ward. I have done all in my power to make her happy, only to have my good intentions treated with childish tantrums and inexcusable behavior."

A decided frost entered her dark eyes at his disparaging words. "Perhaps you would be better served to ask her what she desires, rather than presuming that you know what is best for her."

"But I do know what is best for her," he retorted with an arrogance that obviously rankled the young maiden. He took full pleasure in the taut line of her jaw. Lord knew that she had rankled him often enough. "Which is precisely why her father requested I become her guardian."

Her shoulders squared in a militant manner. "In my experience, gentlemen always presume they are better capable of controlling a lady's life than herself."

"And you do not agree with such sentiment?"

"No."

He stepped close enough to smell the scent of her hair and feel the heat of her satin skin. "So you believe I should simply turn my back on my ward and force her to make her way through the world on her own?"

She shivered, but her gaze never wavered. "Does she not have an income of her own?"

Philip paused, wondering where the minx was attempting to lead him. "A small inheritance currently under my care."

"Then why do you not allow her to establish her own home? She would then no longer be your concern."

A home of her own? Did she think he was daft? He would as soon leave a babe on the streets of

London. "And leave her vulnerable to every lecher and fortune hunter who might pass by? I hardly believe that was what her father would wish."

A surprising flash of pain rippled over her delicate features. "I would think that if her father truly cared for her, he would wish for her to be happy above all things."

With an effort, he hardened his heart against her vulnerability. Of course her father would wish her to be happy. Just as he wanted her to be happy. But first and foremost, he had to ensure that she was securely settled with a suitable husband. Once she was wed, she would realize that everything he was doing was in her own best interest, he assured himself. Perhaps someday she might even thank him.

Fah. She was more likely to sprout wings and fly, he acknowledged dryly. Still, he would do whatever was necessary to save her from her own foolhardy self.

"Happy and secure with a suitable husband," he retorted.

Her expression hardened. "You seem to have an answer for everything."

"Yes." He deliberately stroked his gaze over her stiff features. He would prove that life with a respectable husband was preferable to a life at the mercy of disreputable males. "Of course, I did not seek you out to discuss my ward. You have been most elusive, my dear."

She instinctively stiffened as his tone dropped to an intimate fashion.

"I have been occupied."

"A pity." He reached out to lightly stroke the curve of her lush lower lip. He felt her tremble. "I particularly wished to see you."

"Why?" she croaked.

"Many reasons. To tell you that your hair reminds me of the sunrise, your skin the richest cream, and your eyes a midnight sky." His voice became husky as his hand moved to cup the back of her neck. "And to do this . . ."

With gentle determination he pulled her close; then, lowering his head, he captured her lips in a searching kiss. He felt her stiffen in shock at his blatant intimacy, but wrapping his arm about her waist, he kept her from pulling away.

Beneath his mouth, her lips were as soft as rose petals, with an innocent sweetness that was more seductive than any amount of expertise. Deepening his kiss, his eyes unconsciously slid shut. He had intended to teach her a lesson in the dangers of men, but as her soft form pressed to his own and her lips opened slightly, his thoughts scattered and a piercing pleasure flooded the pit of his stomach.

How small and tender she felt in his arms. How perfectly she curved into his hard frame. Far more perfect than any other woman he had held so close.

His hand moved from her neck to stroke the tender line of her jaw, his heart quickening at her telltale quiver. She was as delicate as a spring blossom with the sweetness of honey. A most potent combination.

The thought flashed through his mind at the same moment he came reluctantly to his senses. Good Lord, what was he doing? He had nearly forgotten that this was no actress ripe for a bit of seduction. This was his ward. An innocent maiden that was entrusted to his care.

With an effort, he disentangled his lips and stepped away. It took a moment to regain his forgotten composure; then he regarded her flushed features with a narrowed gaze.

At least his ploy appeared to have some effect on the stubborn chit, he reassured himself. Her cheeks were flushed while her breath was tortured, as if she had been running for miles.

A trembling hand raised to her reddened lips as she gazed at him with accusing eyes.

"You . . . Why did you do that?"

A hint of amusement entered his silver eyes. "Because I could no longer resist."

"Really, my lord, you are no gentleman."

"I assure you that I am very much a gentleman." He gave a low chuckle. "A gentleman who appreciates the charms of a beautiful lady."

The flush deepened. "Well, I assure you that I do not appreciate being . . . attacked in such a fashion."

"I merely kissed you."

"Much against my will," she charged.

He reached out to stroke her cheek. "I do not recall you struggling. Indeed, you seemed to be quite enjoying yourself."

She jerked from his lingering touch, her eyes almost black with distress. "I was shocked."

"Because I kissed you, or because you enjoyed my kisses?" he demanded softly.

Her startled fear was swiftly replaced by her ready temper at his accusation. "Perhaps the ladies in London consider you irresistible, my lord, but I do not."

He smiled with a smug satisfaction. "Ah . . . We still play the game, eh, Mrs. Smith?"

"You . . ." Words failed her as she glared into his dark countenance; then, as if she could bear no more, she pushed her way past him and fled the hothouse with furious haste.

Philip's smile only widened as he bent down to

retrieve the flower basket that had been forgotten
during the passionate kiss. "Yes, it is coming along
quite nicely," he murmured as he straightened.
"Very nicely, indeed."

Two days later, Bella reluctantly left the sanctuary
of her room and entered the large book-lined library. As with the rest of the estate, the furnishings
were classic in design, with a pretty green-and-ivory-
striped pattern on the small sofas and matching
curtains that covered the floor-length windows. On
the ceiling, a molded plaster displayed the mono-
gram and arms of the Stenhold family.

Bella, however, was in no mood to appreciate her
elegant surroundings. After two days of running
herself haggard in an effort to avoid the annoying
Lord Brasleigh, she was anxious for a brief respite.
Thank goodness the two gentlemen had left early
that morning to view the vicarage. She would at
least have a few hours of uninterrupted peace.

Not that she felt much peace, she acknowledged
as she moved to the window seat and gazed over
the distant lake. Ever since that unforgivable kiss,
her emotions had been in chaos. It was ridiculous.
Although she had never before been kissed, she
could not believe that a simple touching of lips
should cause such turmoil.

But it was undeniable that those brief moments
had been branded upon her brain—the feel of his
lips pressed to her own, the hardness of his body,
and the utterly enticing heat that had flooded
through her blood.

No, she sternly chastised herself. Not again. She
had relived and rehashed those moments in his
arms a hundred times. There was simply no expla-

nation for why she had not struggled to free herself or why her lips had parted as if in invitation for further intimacies. No rational explanation, at any rate.

Just a few more days, she told herself attempting to soothe the panic that always hovered a breath away. Lord Brasleigh would view the estate today, and he would have no further reason to linger. He would be on his way to London, and she would be forever free of his obnoxious presence.

Dwelling on that happy thought, she was suddenly interrupted as the door to the library was pushed open and Lady Stenhold stepped inside. Attired in a rose satin gown, she appeared younger than her years, but it was her searching gaze that had Bella slowly rising to her feet. "Lady Stenhold."

"Here you are, Anna."

The older woman smiled, although Bella was uncomfortably nervous that Lady Stenhold had not missed the pallor of Bella's countenance or the shadows beneath her eyes.

"I wondered where you had disappeared to."

"Did you need anything?"

"Only a bit of company," Lady Stenhold assured her. "I have quite grown accustomed to having someone to share my tea."

Bella's wariness melted beneath the widow's open kindness. "As have I."

"Mrs. Clarke should be along with the tray. Why do you not join me?"

Moving across the room, Bella settled next to her hostess on the sofa. In spite of herself, she couldn't help but make sure that she was still safe. "Lord Blackmar has not yet returned?"

"No. I could hold tea if you prefer to wait for their arrival?"

"Certainly not."

Lady Stenhold studied the heat that rose to Bella's cheeks. "Tell me, Anna, you were not previously acquainted with Lord Brasleigh?"

"N-no," Bella hastily denied. "I have never traveled to London."

"It just seemed . . ." Lady Stenhold's words trailed away as she gave a sudden shrug. "Well, never mind."

Desperately attempting to maintain a measure of her composure, Bella was relieved when the housekeeper entered the room to place a large tray on the table. Rising, the servant glanced toward Lady Stenhold. "Miss Summers is here to see you, my lady."

"Oh." Lady Stenhold gave a blink of surprise. Miss Summers was the daughter of the local vicar, and as a rule was rarely allowed to travel about the countryside without her overbearing father in tow. "Please send her in."

The housekeeper left, and in a moment the short, rather plump young lady attired in a threadbare gray gown entered the room. As always, Bella felt a pang of sympathy for the awkward young maiden with mousy brown hair. She was utterly downtrodden by her father, and was seemingly without friends or relatives to ease her loneliness.

The bully of a vicar could be vastly improved with a bit of humor and kindness, Bella had always thought.

Crossing to the center of the room, Miss Summers bobbed a curtsy.

"Oh, Lady Stenhold, so kind of you to see me," she stammered. "Father absolutely insisted that I call."

Lady Stenhold smiled kindly. "We are always delighted to have the pleasure of your company, Miss Summers."

"So kind." The maiden shifted her attention to Bella, her gaze lingering rather enviously on the lemon muslin gown that she wore. "And Mrs. Smith, what a pretty gown."

"Thank you."

"Father forbids me to wear yellow," she artlessly confessed. "He tells me that it makes me appear to be a pear."

Bella had no trouble imagining the vicar making such a cutting remark, and her tender heart was immediately roused to sympathy. "I should think you would look lovely."

"Oh, no . . ." Miss Summers protested in embarrassment.

"You should wear what pleases you," Bella insisted.

"Father is very particular."

Clearly sensing Bella's desire to inform the young woman that her father was a pompous imbecile, Lady Stenhold diplomatically turned the conversation. "Was there a reason you called today?" she gently inquired.

"Oh, yes. So silly of me. Father wishes to ensure that you will allow the spring fete to be held at Mayfield again this year."

"You may inform the vicar that I should be quite happy to have the fete here. And he may safely leave the details to me."

"Thank you," Miss Summers gushed. "It is always such a lovely occasion."

"It is the least I can do." Lady Stenhold waved a hand toward the tray. "We were just about to enjoy tea. Will you not join us?"

"Oh, no, I couldn't intrude," Miss Summers declined; then as the door abruptly flew open and two large males entered the room, she immediately flushed with nervous confusion. "I . . . oh . . ."

Bella's reaction was no less dramatic. Her face paled even as Lord Brasleigh stepped into the room, and immediately turned to closely examine her delicate countenance and slender form.

Blast.

How the devil did he manage to view any estate so swiftly? Surely he could do no more than gallop past the place before turning back to Mayfield?

Aggravating man.

An awkward silence fell, before Lord Blackmar stepped forward with an engaging smile. "Forgive us, Aunt Caroline. We did not realize that you were entertaining."

"You are welcome," Lady Stenhold insisted. "I wish to introduce you to Miss Summers. Miss Summers, my nephew, Lord Blackmar and his companion, Lord Brasleigh."

"Oh . . ." Miss Summers stammered.

Both gentlemen approached to make their bows.

"Miss Summers," Lord Blackmar dutifully retorted.

Lord Brasleigh, on the other hand, offered one of his most charming smiles as he made her a bow. "A pleasure, Miss Summers."

Clearly overwhelmed by the raven-haired lord breathtakingly attired in top boots and breeches with a blue coat that molded his exquisite form, the poor maiden stumbled backward. "Oh . . ."

"Careful." Lord Brasleigh reached out as Miss Summers hit the tiny table that held a Chinese vase filled with daffodils. He was too late, and becoming tangled in the skirts of her gown, Miss Summers tumbled to the floor, taking the table and vase with her. There was a loud crash and Bella and Lady Stenhold rose to their feet.

"So clumsy of me," Miss Summers whispered in acute embarrassment. "So clumsy."

Quite unexpectedly, it was Lord Brasleigh who rushed to her aid, bending down beside her to tenderly help her to her feet. "Not at all," he denied kindly.

Glancing at the overturned table and shattered vase, Miss Summers gave a small cry. "Oh, I have broken your pretty vase."

"Think nothing of it, my dear," Lady Stenhold insisted.

"Here, allow me." Lord Brasleigh once again bent, righting the table and picking up the shards of the vase. "A most inconveniently placed table."

Miss Summers lifted her hands to her painfully hot cheeks. "No, no. It is all my fault. So clumsy. Please, my lord, do not cut yourself."

"Nonsense." Righting himself, he deposited the shards on the table. "There."

"I am so d-dreadfully sorry," Miss Summers stammered.

In thorough astonishment, Bella watched as Lord Brasleigh produced his handkerchief and lifted Miss Summers's pudgy arm that was wet from the water in the vase.

"Let me dry you off."

With great care, Lord Brasleigh wiped her arm dry, clearly unaware that the poor maiden was about to swoon at his solicitous attentions.

"Oh . . ."

Finished, Lord Brasleigh stepped back with a small smile. "I fear I can do nothing for your gown."

With a flustered motion, Miss Summers waved

her hands. "It will soon dry, thank you. I should be leaving."

"I did not see a carriage when we returned. Are you walking?" Lord Brasleigh demanded.

"Yes, it is only a short distance."

"I shall accompany you."

More flustered than ever, Miss Summers gave a nervous laugh. "There is no need, my lord."

"I will not take no for an answer." In his arrogant fashion, Lord Brasleigh firmly took her arm and began leading the bemused maiden toward the door. "Beautiful ladies should not be walking through the countryside on their own."

There were no further protests as the maiden adoringly allowed herself to be whisked from the room. Just for a moment, Bella attempted to convince herself that Lord Brasleigh was simply acting true to form. As a hardened rogue, he simply could not resist seducing any lady who happened to be near. But she failed to convince herself.

There had been nothing flirtatious in his manner. Instead, he had revealed an innate kindness and generosity of heart that had quite caught her off guard. Had she ever met another gentleman who would have reacted with such compassion?

"Well, I must say that was most elegantly done," Lady Stenhold said, breaking the silence with obvious admiration.

"Yes. Philip has always possessed the oddest sympathy for those ladies most would consider an antidote," Lord Blackmar concluded with a smile.

"A true cavalier," Lady Stenhold stated.

Lord Blackmar shrugged. "Yes. It was really quite amazing to watch the most beautiful debutantes in London vying for his attention only to be passed over for some forgotten miss in the corner."

Bella tried not to listen. She did not want to consider that Lord Brasleigh was not the black-hearted rake she had labeled him. Still, she could not deny that it was a struggle not to admire the gentleman Lord Blackmar was describing.

"I recall his father possessed a similar kindness toward those less fortunate," Lady Stenhold murmured.

"Which is no doubt how he landed himself with Lady Brasleigh."

Lady Stenhold grimaced. "Yes."

"Thank God my own mother possessed the sense to cut my leading strings," Lord Blackmar stated in firm tones. "Poor Philip is forced to cater to that harridan's constant demands."

"Richard," Lady Stenhold protested.

"It is true. She might pretend to be on her deathbed, but she manages to play Philip for a fool. It is little wonder that he has avoided marriage like the plague. He has enough troubles with his mother and, of course, his unruly ward." Unaware that Bella's eyes had widened at the condemning referral to Lord Brasleigh's ward, Lord Blackmar gave a faint bow. "Excuse me. I must change for dinner."

He left the room, and Bella tightened her lips. Unruly? She would like to see how he would react if he were the one about to be hoisted up the aisle. And besides, Lord Brasleigh might be the perfect gentlemen toward his mother and unfortunate misses, but he had revealed a decided lack of sympathy toward his ward.

And as for his behavior toward her since coming to Surrey . . . Well, there was nothing cavalier about it at all.

No, she had no reason to feel a prick of guilt.

None whatsoever.

Five

Seated at the pianoforte in a distant corner, Bella absently plucked out a tune. It was not that she had any desire to display her dubious talent, but she was willing to do whatever necessary to place herself far away from the vicinity of Lord Brasleigh.

She had waited for days for the announcement that the two gentlemen were leaving Surrey. After all, they had no further reason to remain. But rather than rushing from the estate as she desperately hoped, they had continued to linger as if they hadn't a desire in the world to return to London.

It was most aggravating, Bella seethed. For goodness' sakes, she couldn't continue to bolt about the neighborhood as she had for the past week. For one thing, she was weary to the bone from her efforts, and for another, the tenants were beginning to regard her with suspicion as she arrived every day with baskets of food and woolen blankets. No doubt they wondered if she were an overzealous philanthropist or just a bit daft.

Then again, she couldn't simply remain at the estate and leave herself vulnerable to the lecherous advances of Lord Brasleigh.

Oh yes, it was all most aggravating.

As if able to read her very thoughts, the raven-haired gentleman suddenly rose to his feet and determinedly made his way in her direction. That familiar tingle inched down her spine as she instinctively stiffened. Even the knowledge that he possessed a softer side did nothing to lessen his potent danger.

Seemingly unaware of her tension, Lord Brasleigh boldly planted himself next to her seated form, the heat of his thighs searing through her blue gauze gown. "That was lovely," he murmured.

Her hands abruptly clenched in her lap. "Thank you."

"Beethoven?"

"Yes."

Not put off by her overt lack of enthusiasm he bent closer. "Shall I turn the pages for you?" His breath brushed the handful of curls she had left free to frame her face.

"I have finished for the evening." She made a move to rise, only to have his fingers settle on her shoulder and gently keep her in place.

"There is no need to run off. I do not bite."

She froze, wishing that she possessed the nerve to push aside his hand. "You'll forgive me if I do not believe you."

He gave a low chuckle. "Well, perhaps a nibble or two. I particularly prefer the nape of the neck as I hold a woman close in my arms. What do you prefer?"

An evocative image of being held in his arms attempted to rise to mind, but was firmly squashed. "My lord," she muttered in reprimand.

"Very well, Mrs. Smith," he relented with a persuasive smile. "What if I promise to be on my best behavior? Could we not have a simple conversation?"

She refused to be charmed. "I cannot imagine that we have anything to say to each other."

"I know very little about you. Have you always lived in Surrey?"

Her wariness deepened. She had been deliberately vague about her life before arriving at Mayfield. After all, the less anyone knew of her, the fewer lies she had to recall. And until now, he had not seemed particularly interested. She could only hope his curiosity was fleeting. His flirtations were bad enough. She did not need him prying into her past.

"No."

"You are not very forthcoming."

"I have no desire to discuss the past."

"Well, I at least know that you have not been to London," he relentlessly pursued. "I should never have forgotten such a lovely face."

Her unease was briefly forgotten as she felt a surge of distaste at his outrageous words. Really, did he think her a complete buffoon? Even trapped in the depths of the country, she had known that the elusive Lord Brasleigh held no interest in debutantes. Only the most exclusive and sought after Cyprians could stir his attention.

"I should be very surprised if you would have even noticed me," she mocked.

"You are very modest."

"No." She recklessly lifted her head to meet his brilliant silver gaze. "I am simply aware of your reputation, my lord. It is well known that your prefer the lures of actresses to respectable debutantes."

Just for a moment he appeared disconcerted by her words. Clearly he had not expected her to be familiar with the gossip surrounding him. There might even have been a hint of color along the lines of his prominent cheekbones. But predictably, he remained in command of the confrontation.

"I will admit that I prefer ladies who enjoy the pleasures of love without the tedious complications of debutantes."

She would just bet that he did, she acknowledged with a flare of distaste. He might treat Miss Summers with all the consideration of a young lady, but women without the protection of a family were a mere amusement to be enjoyed and then tossed aside.

"Ladies who are dependent upon you for their livelihood and in no position to make demands, you mean?" she demanded in distaste. "Hardly love."

The silver eyes glittered at her sharp accusation. "That is a decidedly low blow, my dear. I assure you that my mistresses have never complained. Indeed, they have all seemed most satisfied."

She refused to blush, although she did not doubt he had fully intended to embarrass her in punishment for her slight upon his charms. "They must be easily satisfied."

He chucked at the thrust, his fingers stroking the soft skin of her shoulders. "What would it take to satisfy you, Mrs. Smith?"

She stiffened as a shocking heat flared through her body. It was anger, nothing else, she hastily reassured herself. That and outrage that he would behave so boldly in front of Lady Stenhold who was being firmly distracted by Lord Blackmar.

"Nothing that you could offer."

"You have not yet heard what I have to offer."

"I am not interested," she muttered.

"Surely a lovely young woman such as yourself cannot be content to play companion to an old woman?" he demanded. "I could give you a home of your own, pretty baubles to wear and of course, the pleasure of my company."

She glared into his handsome countenance. "Pleasure?"

"Of course."

"A pleasure for whom?"

His gaze dropped to her unsteady lips. "For the both of us, I promise."

"I thought I had made it clear that I have no interest in such an arrangement."

He merely gave a click of his tongue. "Such a tease."

Her breath hissed between her clenched teeth. "Good heavens, are you always so persistent?"

"That all depends upon how badly I want something." He shrugged one broad shoulder. "And, of course, we both know that this pretense is no more than a ploy to capture my interest."

A ploy? For goodness' sakes, the man possessed enough arrogance to fill all of England. "I would suggest that you change the topic of conversation, my lord, unless you wish to have your face slapped," she threatened darkly.

The fingers roamed the curve of her neck. "Ah . . . I do like a woman of spirit, Mrs. Smith."

She jerked from his touch. "And I like a gentleman who knows how to behave as a gentleman."

"I can behave any way you like." He bent even closer. "Shall I come to your room tonight and prove it?"

She gasped in disbelief. "Certainly not."

"Then come to my room."

"No."

He straightened slowly, a hint of steely determination etched on his dark features. "Very well. We shall continue our game another day or two, but I promise, Mrs. Smith, by the end of the week you will be mine."

With a faint bow, Lord Brasleigh turned to stroll back toward Lady Stenhold, leaving Bella more shaken than angry. He seemed so . . . relentless. So confident. How was she to convince him to leave her alone? She had to discover some means.

It was that or fleeing once again.

There was a definite hint of spring in the air as Bella and Lady Stenhold stepped from the small church. Bella sucked in a deep breath of the flower-scented air. It was a welcome relief to be standing in the fresh air after two tedious hours of enduring the droning chastisements from the vicar on the sins of mankind.

Beside her, Lady Stenhold glanced toward the portly vicar who was hovering beside the church with smug self-importance. "I do wish the vicar would devote as much passion to tending to his flock as to condemning them."

Bella could only shudder at the thought. The vicar would no doubt bully and terrify his flock if he took it into his thick head to take an interest in their personal lives. "He is a rather stern man," she carefully retorted.

"He is a wretched bully." Lady Stenhold was not nearly so discrete. "I pity his daughter."

"Yes." Bella turned to glance at Miss Summers, her heart giving a queer leap at the sight of Lord Brasleigh standing at her side.

As always, he was impeccably attired, his fitted

coat so snug she could easily discern the muscles of his broad chest. It was a sight that appeared to delight Miss Summers, and she giggled with pleasure at something he was saying.

For no reason at all the sight decidedly annoyed Bella.

Lady Stenhold, on the other hand, appeared inordinately pleased. "I must say that she has quite bloomed beneath Lord Brasleigh's attentions. I have never seen her appear so lovely."

Bella's features unconsciously hardened. "He is a most practiced rogue."

"So I have noted," Lady Stenhold agreed in dry tones, her shrewd gaze abruptly turning back to Bella. "Is he . . . troubling you, Anna?"

Bella was caught off guard by the abrupt question. Oh, how she would love to confess that the insufferable man was not only troubling her, but that he had insulted her in the most shameful manner. She had no doubt that Lady Stenhold would be deeply shocked and soon would have him tossed from her estate. But always in the back of her mind was the fear that such an action might enrage the man to the point of retaliation. She could not have him seeking more information on the mysterious Mrs. Smith to enact his revenge.

So instead she swallowed her hasty words and forced herself to give a small shrug. "He is simply the type of gentleman who feels the need to flirt with every lady he encounters."

"Perhaps," Lady Stenhold murmured in skeptical tones. "You do know that I would request Richard to return to London with Lord Brasleigh if need be."

Bella smiled with genuine gratitude. "Thank you, but I am certain they will soon be leaving. Besides, it must be pleasant for you to have the company of your nephew."

Lady Stenhold considered her words for a moment before an odd expression flitted over her lined countenance. "Richard has been decidedly elusive. It is almost as if he is avoiding a comfortable chat with me. Very odd."

Bella had been so enwrapped in her own troubles that she had not taken much notice of Lord Blackmar. Now she regarded Lady Stenhold with a frown. "Is something wrong, do you think?"

Lady Stenhold tapped a gloved finger to her chin. "I am uncertain. I shall no doubt discover the truth in time."

Unsure what was stewing in the older woman's mind, Bella was distracted as Miss Summers suddenly appeared beside them. "Good morning, Lady Stenhold. Mrs. Smith."

"Good morning, Miss Summers," Lady Stenhold greeted warmly. "Do you not look lovely?"

The maiden blushed, glancing down at her gown of a surprising shade of pale green. It was the first occasion that Bella had ever seen her in anything but her drab gray. "Thank you."

"I do not think that I have ever seen you wear such a pretty gown."

An expression of happiness illuminated her round face, lending an air that was most becoming. "Is it not lovely?" she breathed. "Lord Brasleigh happened to mention to Father that the bishop particularly preferred women to wear gaily colored gowns. He says that God would not have given nature such beautiful colors if he wished to view only black and gray."

It was no doubt a devious lie, but not even Bella could condemn Lord Brasleigh's deception. He had performed no less than a miracle in swaying the vicar from swathing his daughter in ugly gray. More importantly, he had also brought an unfamiliar sparkle to her eyes.

Lady Stenhold was clearly of the same opinion as a small smile curved her mouth. "A very wise man."

"Yes," Miss Summers swiftly agreed.

Lady Stenhold regarded her in a coy fashion. "You seem to be enjoying the company of Lord Brasleigh."

"He is so very kind." Miss Summers clasped her hands in a reverent motion. "He never makes me feel stupid or clumsy."

"Of course not. You are a very accomplished young lady."

Miss Summers gave a shake of her head. "I wish it were so, my lady, but I have always known that I was a sore disappointment to my father. He no doubt wishes that I could have been more like my mother. She always seemed to know precisely what to say and how to make others feel comfortable."

Bella felt a surge of compassion. Having lost her own mother at a young age, she knew precisely how difficult it was to be raised in the shadow of memories. A young girl could not help but compare herself to her mother and find herself wanting, especially without the loving support of a father.

"You have your own strengths, my dear," Lady Stenhold insisted.

Miss Summers's smile returned. "That is what Lord Brasleigh tells me."

"Then he is quite right."

There was a sound across the way and the three ladies turned to discover the vicar waving his arm in an imperative manner.

"Oh, Father is ready to leave," Miss Summers exclaimed. "I must make sure his luncheon is prepared. Excuse me." With a hasty dip, the maiden rushed away to join her father.

Bella watched her retreat with a faint frown. There was no doubt that Miss Summers appeared decidedly improved by Lord Brasleigh's efforts. Still, her own feelings toward the gentleman remained a tangle of anger and suspicion. How could he be such a noble gentleman one moment and an out-and-out cad the next?

"Lord Brasleigh seems to have found favor with one lady in the neighborhood," Lady Stenhold pointed out with a narrowed gaze upon Bella's pale countenance.

Bella's lips thinned. "As I said, he is a very accomplished flirt."

"Still, it is kind of him to make such an effort with poor Miss Summers. She has had precious few gentlemen offer her such attention."

"I only hope that she is not hurt," Bella muttered.

Lady Stenhold reached out to pull Bella's arm through her own. "I am certain that all will be well."

"If you say so."

"Come along, my dear."

Negligently standing in the shadows of the church, Philip watched with a faint smile as Lady Stenhold and Bella climbed into the carriage. He had not missed Bella's covert glance in his direction, nor the faint hint of relief as she realized he was still present.

He had no doubt she intended to seek her private chambers the moment she returned to the estate. Lady Stenhold always rested after church, and the maiden would not want to risk being alone with him. But Philip was already one move ahead of her, and before the carriage had even begun to move, he had given a faint wave to Pudding and was swiftly retrieving his mount.

Within moments, he was away from the church and cutting through the back meadows and fields that would lead to Mayfield. Bella had eluded him for the past week. Today would be different.

Unconsciously humming a tune, Philip urged his mount to a gallop. The sun was warm on his face and a faint breeze carried the scent of clover. A beautiful day for a ride, but Philip did not allow himself to linger. Instead, he cut a direct path to the estate, barely slowing his horse to a trot as he entered the stables. Then, leaving his mount in the care of a groom, he crossed to the gardens to enter through the side door. He did, however, pause long enough to pluck a perfect rose from a nearby bush.

Once inside, he was careful to check that there were no servants about to view his entrance. With graceful stealth, he climbed the steps and made his way to Bella's room. For a moment, he paused to inspect the tidy chamber, noting the obvious lack of possessions scattered about. He had known that she was unable to take many things on her hurried flight and could only shake his head in bewilderment. What maiden with the least amount of sense would flee the lavish existence he had offered her for a life as a common servant?

Granted, her place with Lady Stenhold was less than onerous, but it was still one that was far from her position as his ward. Or as Monsieur LeMont's wife. She was clearly incapable of making suitable decisions for her own future.

Philip settled his tall form on the wide bed. Miss Bella Lowe might possess more spirit than he had originally suspected, but he knew that his constant attentions were wearing down her staunch courage. It would take little more to have her scurrying back to his estate. Beginning today he intended to bellow the flames a bit higher.

A rather startling flare of anticipation raced through his body as he heard the sound of light footsteps approaching. He could not deny he was enjoying this game with his ward. Perhaps more than he had enjoyed anything in a very long time.

Watching the door open, Philip was silent as Bella entered and firmly shut the door behind her. Then, with an audible breath of relief, she slowly turned only to freeze in horror.

"You . . ."

With his most engaging grin, Philip held out the rose he had picked. "I brought you this."

A sharp color flooded her cheeks at his audacity. "How dare you come in here? Do you mean to create a scandal?"

Unrepentant, he allowed a slow smile to curve his mouth. "You know what I wish."

"This is too much, sir." She stomped her foot in childish rage. "Leave this room immediately."

Slowly rising to his feet, he deliberately strolled until he was towering over her trembling form. "But I have no desire to leave. And I believe that if you would only be honest, you would admit that you too have no desire for me to leave."

"You . . ." Her nose flared with fury. "I can only presume that you received a head wound during the war, my lord. Or else you are simply daft. There could be no other excuse for your inability to comprehend the word *no.*"

Philip chuckled at her fierce tone. "Thankfully my head made it through the war without incident, as did the rest of me. Of course, if you doubt my word you could always examine me yourself."

Her chest heaved in fury. A most enticing sight, Philip was forced to conclude.

"The only thing I wish is for you to leave my chamber."

"Come, come, my love. This game has gone on quite long enough. I have played my part, and now it is time for you to play yours."

"If you do not leave, I shall scream," she threatened, her tone unsteady.

He gave a slow shake of his head. "Do not be absurd, my dear. We both knew this moment would come the moment our eyes met. It is destiny."

Philip watched in fascination as color stained her pale countenance. She had never appeared lovelier.

"I will scream, and Lady Stenhold will throw you out of her house," she assured him.

"Did you know that your eyes become the darkness of an Italian sky at midnight when you are angry?" he murmured softly.

His compliment only fueled her ire. "My lord . . ."

"Philip," he interrupted softly.

"What?"

"I wish to hear my name upon your lips."

"Sir," she retorted in stern tones.

"I see I shall have to convince you." Reaching up, he framed her tiny face with gentle hands. "Say my name."

"No . . ." she breathed, her eyes wide and dark with emotion.

Allowing the exquisite tension to build, Philip slowly lowered his head, capturing her lips with masterful pressure.

Intent on plunder, Philip meant to prove just how vulnerable she was to a man intent on seduction. But once again, he was caught off guard as his mouth encountered the sweet tenderness of her lips. Heavens above, they seemed to melt beneath the heat of his touch, molding to his own with a bewitching innocence. With a low groan, his hands dropped to stroke her neck and down the modest line of her bodice. His kiss was meant to be a punishment. A lesson to frighten her into marriage. But as he felt her soft body press closer to his own, all thoughts of punishment were vanquished by a flare of searing heat.

His heart gave a savage kick as he expertly parted her lips and deepened the kiss. He wanted to drown in her seductive innocence. To tutor her in the delights of passion.

His hands moved once again, rounding her slender waist to press her to his stirring thighs. With one smooth movement, he could have her off her feet and lying upon the bed. He would slowly strip away the bothersome dress and kiss the rose-petal tips of her breasts to poignant desire. He would ease apart those slender legs. . . .

"Philip . . ." she whispered softly. "Oh, Philip."

With the shock of a bucket of cold water being tossed upon his head, Philip abruptly realized what he was doing.

Good gads! Had he completely lost his wits? He was despicable, he told himself. No, worse than despicable. He was as bad as any lecher he was supposedly attempting to protect Bella from.

Untangling himself from her clinging arms, he

gave a sharp shake of his head. He had been a fool to come to this room, he chastised himself. No, more than a fool. Frightening the chit into marriage was one thing, but to actually consider laying her upon the bed and . . .

Philip felt a shudder wrack his body. Whatever his motives, he had behaved in a shameful manner. And it did not help to realize that the heat that had sparked between them still smoldered in the pit of his stomach.

Thoroughly repulsed with himself, Philip abruptly stepped past the bemused maiden and stormed from the room.

He did not consider the realization that far from being frightened, she had responded with trembling enthusiasm. Or that he had managed to coerce her into saying his name. His only thought was that he had come perilously close to seducing his own ward.

Six

As he left the room, Philip was no more ashamed and bewildered than Bella.

Scrubbing an angry hand over her throbbing lips, she sought to banish the searing heat that had flooded to the very tips of her toes. She had been beyond foolish. It did not matter that she had been caught off guard. Or that Lord Brasleigh was obviously a master of seduction. He had pressed his lips to hers, and she had melted like the most susceptible schoolgirl.

Why? Why did this gentleman possess the ability to make her blood rush and her stomach quiver?

Could it be that she was so shallow she could be vulnerable to a handsome face and practiced skill, no matter how contemptible their motives?

With a shudder of revulsion, Bella leaned against her dressing stand; then, as another wave of self-loathing coursed through her, she grasped a tiny figurine and hurled it across the room. Although she would no doubt later regret her impulsive action, for the moment she thoroughly enjoyed the sound of shattering glass. It somehow echoed the feeling of her own shattered belief in passion and love.

How innocent she had been to presume that passion could only be inspired when love was present. She had never realized the power of a man's touch or her own unruly response to a practiced kiss.

Fool. Fool. Fool.

On the point of tossing yet another figurine, Bella was halted as the door opened and a maid nervously entered the chambers. The young servant's eyes widened at the sight of the broken glass. "Oh."

With an effort, Bella drew herself upright, although there was nothing she could do about the high color still staining her cheeks. "Hello, Mary."

"What has occurred?"

"What has occurred? Men, that's what has occurred," Bella seethed out loud.

Mary gave a startled blink. "Men?"

"Who else could infuriate a reasonable woman? They are all overbearing, selfish boors, and I assure you the world would be a better place without them."

The maid was clearly shocked. No doubt, she had been properly trained to believe there was nothing more sacred than capturing and pleasing a husband. She appeared deeply distressed by such a lack of respect.

"Oh, you cannot mean that, ma'am."

"I assure you that I do," Bella snapped, placing all her current troubles and woes directly onto Lord Brasleigh's shoulders. If the impossible man had remained in London where he belonged, she would have been perfectly happy and secure.

"But surely . . ." Mary stammered to an uncomfortable halt.

"What?"

"Well, surely every lady desires a gentleman to love and protect her?"

Bella gave a loud snort. "You mean a gentleman to order her about and control her life without regard to her own feelings?"

Mary gave a small shake of her head, obviously not as intimately acquainted with the treachery of men as Bella. "Gentlemen were meant to care for women."

"Fah." Bella thought of her own father's disregard and then Lord Brasleigh's determination to rid himself of her. "I am perfectly capable of caring for myself, and I have no desire to be bothered by the demands of a supposed gentleman."

Mary heaved a wistful sigh. "I should like to have a husband someday."

Bella resisted the urge to inform the gullible maid that a husband would no doubt only add to her burden of a life of servitude. Girls liked to dream of love, not of being commanded to cook and clean and raise the numerous children with as little trouble to the husband as possible.

Besides, however cynical she might feel at the moment, she could not entirely give up on love. Wasn't that why she had fled rather than wed a complete stranger?

"Well, perhaps you shall be fortunate enough to discover a husband who does not treat you as part of his property," she muttered. "But I should not hold out much hope."

"You are simply upset, Mrs. Smith." Mary sent her a soothing smile.

"Yes, I am," Bella admitted with a rueful grimace. "And I have no right to take my ill humor out on you, Mary. Forgive me."

Mary waved aside the apology. "It is nothing. I suppose you are angry with Lord Brasleigh?"

Bella froze. Had the maid seen the two of them together? "Why would you think that this has anything to do with Lord Brasleigh?"

"It is just that . . . Well, I have noticed the manner in which he watches you," Mary hesitantly explained. "He cannot take his gaze from you when you enter the room."

Bella's expression hardened. Blast the devilish lord. Now he had even caused the servants to notice his unwelcome attentions. Soon she would be the source of gossip throughout the neighborhood. "I wish he would go away."

"Oh, you should not say such a thing, miss. He is a fine gentleman. Always so polite and generous to the staff. Not at all like most London nobs." A coy expression crossed the maid's countenance. "And so handsome."

"He is a . . ." Bella reluctantly bit back her condemning words. There was no use in fueling the maid's avid curiosity about her relationship with Lord Brasleigh. "It is of no importance. Was there something that you needed, Mary?"

"Lady Stenhold has requested that you join her in the front drawing room."

Bella heaved a sigh. She wanted nothing more than to lock herself in her rooms and brood for the remainder of the day. "Did she say why?"

"No, ma'am."

"Very well," Bella conceded, knowing it was impossible to hide forever. "Tell her I will join her in a moment."

"Of course." With a bob, the maid left the room.

Bella lifted shaking hands to make sure her curls were still safely tucked atop her head. There was little use in postponing the inevitable, she decided. Although Lady Stenhold was far from demanding, she was tenacious. With a regretful glance around the sweetly silent room, she turned to make her way into the hall and then to the sweeping staircase. On the last stair, she prepared to turn toward the front drawing room when the sound of approaching footsteps had her cowardly darting behind a large potted plant. A familiar tingle warned her who was approaching. Peeking through the branches, she was not surprised to spot Lord Brasleigh abruptly appearing from a side door and heading directly into the library.

At his entrance, Bella could see Lord Blackmar abruptly rising to his feet. "Good lord, Bras, what has occurred?"

Knowing she should slip away before she was discovered, Bella was halted as Lord Brasleigh roughly growled, "My bloody ward. That's what is the matter."

"I believe this calls for a drink," Lord Blackmar retorted, easily noting the dark expression marring Philip's countenance.

Philip did not protest. He was beyond hiding his seething emotions. Not that he intended to reveal the cause for his current distemper, he acknowledged wryly. How did he confess that he longed to toss his ward onto the nearest bed and drown in her sweetness?

"Several drinks," he rasped, accepting the proffered glass of brandy and downing it in one gulp.

"Here." Pudding had wisely brought the bottle and swiftly refilled Philip's glass. Then, tilting his head to one side, he regarded his friend with a narrowed gaze. "Would you like to share what has you in such a foul mood?"

Philip's features twisted. "I am merely annoyed with the entire bloody mess. I should be in London enjoying myself, not acting like a fool in the midst of this godforsaken country."

Pudding regarded him for a long moment before allowing a rather mysterious smile to curve his lips. "I had quite convinced myself you were enjoying your role as the debauched seducer."

A flame of heat scorched Philip's cheeks at the accusation. It was far too close for comfort. "What the deuce are you implying?" he demanded.

Pudding raised his hands in a vague motion. "Well, I have never seen you so enwrapped with a lady before—even those you actually intended to seduce. Certainly Miss Ravel never received such attentions."

"Fah." Philip refused to acknowledge that the beautiful actress had never captured his attention as Bella had. "I assure you, this all has been a game, nothing more."

"A very enticing game, no doubt," Pudding purred.

Philip rewarded his friend with a glare. "Pudding."

The brilliantly attired gentleman gave a sudden laugh. "Well, even you have to admit that she is unreasonably beautiful."

"She is also unreasonably stubborn, ill behaved, and without the least amount of common sense."

Pudding raised his brows at Philip's fierce tone. "You knew that before we came," he pointed out with unshakable logic. "So what has you in such a twit?"

Philip abruptly banged his glass down onto a nearby bookshelf. "She should be terrified by now. Any young maiden with the least sensibilities would have realized how dangerous her position is and have fled to the safety of her guardian."

"So why hasn't she?"

Philip breathed out a harsh sigh. "She clearly believes she is capable of overcoming any situation."

That mysterious smile returned to Pudding's lips. "Perhaps she is."

"You are determined to end up her groom," he threatened.

"Not I."

Philip shook his head. "I have all but ravished her, and still she refuses to accept the truth."

"Clearly she feels being forced into marriage worse than being ravished."

"Nonsense," Philip denied, without allowing himself to give thought to Pudding's accusation. "Every young maiden dreams of acquiring a husband. She is merely so determined to flaunt my authority, it has blinded her."

"You two seem well matched."

"What does that mean?"

Pudding slowly sipped his brandy, carefully noting the color that came and went in Philip's thin face. "It seems that your own determination to force your will upon Miss Lowe has blinded you to all but your need to win."

Philip stiffened at the accusation. "It is her father's will, not mine. He entrusted her to my care. Do you suppose he would wish for me to allow her to become a mere servant?"

"No," Pudding conceded, although that devious twinkle never left his eyes. "No doubt he would wish her to be properly wed."

Philip unconsciously clenched his fists. The flare of distaste for handing her over to another only hardened his determination. The sooner he was free of Miss Bella Lowe the better. "And that is precisely what I intend to see occur."

"What will you do?"

Philip frowned. "For the moment I will continue with my plan."

"If it continues to fail?"

"I will tie her in a sack and drag her up the aisle," Philip responded bluntly.

Pudding gave a sharp laugh. "That I should love to see. No doubt the groom would be quite flattered to have his bride arrive in such a fashion."

Philip's thoughts turned to Andre LeMont and then naturally to his dragon of a mother. His features twisted into a grimace. "It might frighten LeMont, but it would not disturb his mother. She would personally force Miss Lowe down the aisle if it ensured she would receive her settlement." His lips twisted. "Although, I must admit that while I initially felt a measure of pity for Miss Lowe to be saddled with such a relative as Madam LeMont, I begin to suspect that she will have the harridan cowed within a month."

Something in his tone had Pudding regarding him with a probing gaze. "Has something occurred that you are not sharing?"

Philip abruptly turned from that knowing gaze, uncomfortably aware that a guilty flush was staining his cheeks. "Nothing beyond the fact that I am anxious to return to London and Miss Ravel. She at least knows how to be with a gentleman without attempting to drive him to Bedlam."

Still behind the potted plant, Bella struggled to keep her shaking knees holding her upright. The shock that had held her in silent disbelief for the past several moments was slowly boiling to a fury she had never before experienced.

He knew. He had known all along.

The . . . lout.

He had somehow managed to track her to Surrey, and rather than confront her like a decent gentleman, he had instead devised this loathsome ploy to frighten her into marriage. Her hand pressed to her trembling lips as she recalled his suggestive words, his lingering touches, and those searing kisses.

Heaven above, he had made such a fool of her. Such a bloody fool.

Why hadn't she suspected? Why hadn't she realized that his arrival in Surrey was far too coincidental for mere chance?

With an effort, she blinked back the tears of fury and humiliation.

It was too late to regret her blind stupidity. Now, she had to concentrate on what to do.

Every part of her quivered with the need to march into the library and slap Lord Brasleigh's arrogant face. But the knowledge that she would be letting him off all too easily kept her behind the plant.

Once he realized that she was aware of his horrid trick, he would no doubt haul her to London and down the aisle just as he had threatened. He would not even feel a twinge of remorse at his reprehensible behavior. No, she would obviously have to flee once again. But first . . . First she intended to teach Lord Brasleigh a severe lesson in playing her for a fool.

Long moments passed as she brooded upon the best means of exacting her revenge. Various plots were considered and dismissed; then at last a notion so simple and yet so daring slowly bloomed in the depths of her mind.

What better means of punishment than to neatly turn the tables on him? He hoped to frighten her into submission with his blatant seduction. What if, instead, she pretended to fall madly in love with him? He would be the one who would appear the fool and hopefully spend a few sleepless nights. After that . . . Well, she would worry about fleeing after she had assured herself that Lord Brasleigh was properly punished.

Squaring her shoulders, she stepped from behind the plant, intending to mount the stairs and return to her chambers. She had completely dismissed the reason she had come downstairs in the first place. But she had barely taken two steps when Mary abruptly appeared. "Mrs. Smith, Lady Stenhold is still awaiting you in the drawing room."

Bella swallowed a sigh of exasperation. Of course. How could she have forgotten poor Lady Stenhold? Her plan would have to wait for now. "Thank you, Mary."

Doing her best to calm her tangled emotions, Bella made her way to the drawing room. Her efforts, however, were not wholly successful as Lady Stenhold watched her enter the crimson-and-gold room with raised brows. "Oh, Anna . . . Are you not well?"

Bella forced a stiff smile. "I am fine."

"You appear flushed."

She gave the first lie that came to mind. "I rather hurried down the stairs."

Lady Stenhold leaned forward, clearly not convinced. "Are you sure it is nothing else?"

Bella suppressed a hysterical urge to laugh. What would the older woman say if she knew that Lord

Brasleigh had come to Surrey to terrify his own ward into marriage? And that she was now prepared to pretend that she was in love with a gentleman that she detested above all others? No doubt she would have the lot of them tossed from her home.

"What do you mean?"

"Lord Brasleigh has not been troubling you?"

"No . . ." Bella gave a shake of her head, desperately hoping that Mary had not confided her suspicions to her mistress. At the moment, she wanted nothing interfering with her plans. "Not at all."

"Are you certain?"

"Quite certain."

There was a short pause. "Very well."

"Did you wish to see me?" Bella hurried to change the subject.

"Yes. I was just thinking that as long as we have guests, we should offer some sort of entertainment."

It was not at all what Bella had been expecting. "Oh?"

"I was thinking we might arrange a ball."

Bella's heart sank. The last thing she wished was to be surrounded by hundreds of guests. Especially when there was always the remote possibility she might be recognized. "Really?"

Lady Stenhold appeared taken aback by her decided lack of enthusiasm. "Does the idea not please you?"

A stab of guilt pierced Bella's heart at the older woman's barely hidden disappointment. "It is hardly my concern," she murmured.

"Of course it is. You are a guest in this house," Lady Stenhold insisted. "If the thought of frivolity is disturbing, then I will certainly not pursue the notion."

"That is very kind, but I could not possibly intrude upon your entertainments," Bella desperately urged. "I shall be quite happy to remain in my chambers during the ball."

Lady Stenhold frowned. "Absurd."

"But . . ."

"If you will not attend the ball, then I shall simply not arrange it."

Bella gazed at the face that had become so dear to her, before slowly giving a wry shake of her head. The lady was an expert at getting her way with her gentle insistence. "Then I shall be happy to join you."

Lady Stenhold beamed with satisfaction. "Excellent. I shall begin making the arrangements at once. Of course, I must warn you that it will be nothing elaborate. Just a few neighbors and friends."

"I am certain it will be lovely." Realizing that the older woman had accomplished what she wished, Bella prepared to make her escape. The upcoming ball would be a worry for another day. At the moment, she had more than enough troubles upon her plate. "Now, if you will excuse me, I have a few matters to attend to."

Seven

There appeared to be an inordinate amount of white skin.

Leaning forward, Bella regarded her plunging neckline in the mirror with a decided flare of unease. It was one thing to request her maid to alter the numerous gowns that Lady Stenhold had insisted upon giving her. It was quite another to actually appear downstairs attired as a . . . a common courtesan.

Stop it, Bella Lowe, she scolded herself. The rose-patterned French silk was certainly more daring and sophisticated than she was accustomed to wearing. And her maid had been unfortunately enthusiastic in lowering the neckline. But there was nothing precisely indecent about the gown. Indeed, there was no doubt that if she were in London, her attire would not even raise a brow.

Besides, her gown was the least of her concerns, she reminded herself sternly. She should be concentrating on how best to begin her campaign against Lord Brasleigh, not worrying over the decided draft in the front of her dress.

With an effort, she turned her thoughts to the problem at hand. It would be difficult, she had al-

ready conceded. She would have to be subtle
enough not to alert Lord Brasleigh that she had
discovered the truth, and yet bold enough to make
him squirm. Hardly an easy task for a woman who
knew as much about gentlemen as she knew about
the strange creatures that swam in the depths of the
ocean.

Giving a slight shake of her head, Bella forced
herself to square her shoulders and take a deep
breath. Ready or not, it was time to make her appearance downstairs. With considerable effort, she
crossed toward the door of her chamber and
stepped into the hall. It took another moment to
conjure the nerve to make her way to the staircase
and down to the main floor.

Entering the lower hall, Bella headed toward the
front drawing room only to come to a halt as she
caught sight of the raven-haired gentleman in the
library. Seated in a wing chair, Lord Brasleigh was
busily studying the large book laid open on his lap.
Her gaze narrowed as she studied his chiseled profile before moving down to the fitted emerald coat
and silver waistcoat.

An odd tremor raced through her body as she
reluctantly acknowledged that he was a handsome
devil. Far more handsome than any other gentleman she had ever encountered.

Not that being handsome and far too practiced
in seducing women in any way compensated for his
wretched behavior, she assured herself. No gentleman could be so handsome or charming as to com-
pensate for that.

Sending up a swift prayer that her courage did
not fail her, Bella determinedly stepped into the
room, pretending to come to a surprised halt as
Lord Brasleigh politely rose to his feet.

"Oh . . . Lord Brasleigh." She batted her lashes in his direction.

Just for a moment his gaze skimmed over her altered gown, lingering on the plunging neckline far too long for comfort. Bella stifled the urge to cover herself with her hands. Then surprisingly, a flare of color touched his high cheekbones, and an unreadable expression descended upon his elegant features. "Mrs. Smith, please join me."

"Oh, I do not wish to intrude."

That practiced smile curved his lips. "You are quite aware that I treasure our moments together."

Treasure? Fah. He could not wait to unload her on the first witless buffoon who would take a bride. "Absurd man." She gave a shrill giggle. "I simply wished to find a book to read."

He gave a startled blink at her antics. "Perhaps I could help?"

"I do not know. What would you suggest?"

"Something that stirs a young lady's blood?" He slipped into character as his voice lowered to a husky pitch. *"Romeo and Juliet,* or perhaps *Anthony and Cleopatra?"*

"Ill-fated love, my lord?" she asked in coy tones.

"Love that was willing to set aside the restrictions of society. That is true passion."

She once again batted her lashes, feeling like the veriest fool. How did any maiden enjoy behaving in such a ridiculous manner? "A pity that it so often ends in tragedy."

"Not always." He moved closer, but there was a decidedly wary glint in his eyes. "We could prove that passion has its share of happy endings."

She felt a flare of wry humor as she recalled his earlier complaints that he was desperate to return to ladies who did not drive him batty. She would show him just how batty she could drive him.

She widened her eyes and gave a faint pout. "But surely you are anxious to return to London?"

"No more anxious than I am to hold you in my arms," he smoothly lied.

She watched as his gaze narrowed, no doubt awaiting her furious set-down to his bold words. Instead, Bella glanced up at him through tangled lashes. "You would remain for me?"

A gathering frown tugged at his brows at her breathless words. "But, of course."

"What of your mistress in London?"

"What is she to us?"

Bella leaned deliberately forward. "Is she very beautiful?"

His gaze skimmed over her pale countenance before dipping with seeming fascination to her neckline. "Not as beautiful as you."

Bella resisted the urge to bat him on the nose with her fan. Hadn't she requested her bodice to be lowered for precisely this purpose? "You think me beautiful?"

His gaze slowly rose to closely scrutinize her set features. "Of course. What gentleman would not find you breathtaking? Hair as brilliant as gold, skin as rich as cream, and lips that beg for a man's kiss."

Until this morning she would have blushed with embarrassment at his deliberately provocative words. Now she summoned a brilliant smile and tapped his chest with her fan. "Oh, sir. You always seem to know precisely what to say."

His frown deepened at her odd behavior. Reaching up, he grasped her slender wrist and raised it to study the lacy concoction in her hand. "I see you have my fan."

She did not tell him that she had scoured the garden until she found where she had tossed it. "Yes. I fear that I never did properly thank you."

"No," he retorted in dry tones. "You did everything but throw it back in my face."

She could hardly deny the truth of his accusation, so she heaved a faint sigh. "Yes. Very ungracious of me."

Dropping her wrist, Lord Brasleigh regarded her for a long, silent moment. "Are you quite well, Mrs. Smith?"

"But, of course. Why do you ask?"

Her seeming innocence did nothing to ease the suspicion carved into his handsome countenance. "Until this moment there has always been a distinct frost in the air when I was near. Now . . . Something seems different."

Bella knew that she would have to be careful. She wanted to prolong his suffering as long as possible. "Perhaps I have realized that I was behaving rather foolishly."

"Oh?" Something flashed deep in his silver eyes.

A thrill of power raced through her as she stepped closer to his large frame. "You must understand that it has been quite some time since a gentleman has revealed an interest in me."

She sensed him stiffening at her soft words. "I find that difficult to believe."

"I have always lived quietly," she pointed out. She had to have some excuse for supposedly desiring a gentleman who had treated her with such a shocking lack of respect. "There have been few opportunities to meet gentlemen. I must admit that you frightened me."

A guarded expression descended upon his dark features. "That was not my intention."

Liar, Bella inwardly seethed. That was precisely his intention. "I suppose you must think me very missish."

He regarded her for another long moment. "I am uncertain what to think," he admitted slowly.

Bella gave a flutter of her fan, but before she could utter a word, the decidedly plump form of Lord Blackmar entered the room. Bella instinctively stepped away from Lord Brasleigh as she regarded the intruder attired in a shocking yellow coat.

"Hi, ho, Bras." Lord Blackmar turned toward Bella and offered her an elegant leg. "Mrs. Smith. Am I intruding?"

Lord Brasleigh's familiar mocking expression returned. "Would it matter?"

Lord Blackmar smiled in a lazy fashion. "Not at all. How charming you look this evening, Mrs. Smith."

Although Lord Blackmar was as elegant and sophisticated as Lord Brasleigh, Bella felt none of the prickly unease she felt in her guardian's presence. Indeed, if he were not in devious companionship with Lord Brasleigh, she might even have enjoyed his sharp wit. "Thank you, Lord Blackmar. And you are as brilliant as ever."

Lord Blackmar chuckled as he glanced down at his yellow attire. "My little joke upon society, Mrs. Smith."

"Oh?"

He shrugged. "I have always known that I could never cut a dash such as Brasleigh or Challmond or Wickton. So I devised a means of creating my own stir among the ton. If I could not be irresistible, then I would be remarkable."

Bella could not help but smile at his blunt revelation. It was true he could never claim the potent appeal of Lord Brasleigh, but he was obviously wise enough to realize that the bored ton would be intrigued with his audacious manner. "Very clever."

"Yes, well, I am a rather clever bloke," he informed her with a wicked smile. "As you would know if Bras were not so beastly selfish as to devour the lion's share of your time."

Lord Brasleigh smoothly moved closer to Bella, his smile dry. "I have no desire to be cut out by a notorious rogue."

"Notorious?" Lord Blackmar protested.

"I urge you, Mrs. Smith, to avoid the attentions of Lord Blackmar with assiduous care. The streets of London are littered with the broken hearts of ladies he has loved and cast aside."

Lord Blackmar gave a loud snort, his lips twitching. "I fear you have me quite mistaken with some other rogue, Bras," he retorted in pointed tones.

"Nonsense." Lord Brasleigh lifted his raven brows. "Should you not be with your aunt in the drawing room?"

"She is not down yet, and I was seeking a bit of entertainment."

"You shall have to seek your entertainment elsewhere," Lord Brasleigh informed him in tart tones.

Lord Blackmar merely smiled. "But I am enjoying my entertainment here."

Lord Brasleigh stepped forward. "Elsewhere."

The two gentlemen regarded each other in silence for a long moment; then a mysterious smile suddenly curved Lord Blackmar's lips. "Be at ease, Bras. I am going." He turned to bow toward the silent Bella. "Until later, my dear."

Watching until the gentleman sauntered from the room, Bella slowly turned to regard Lord Brasleigh with a wide-eyed gaze. "You were very abrupt with your friend."

"He was being a nuisance." Lord Brasleigh dismissed his friend with a wave of his hand; then with obvious effort, he summoned a seductive smile. Bella felt a tingle of anticipation as she prepared to resume their game.

"Now, I believe we were about to choose a book?"

She ducked her head in a shy motion. "Do you not think that we should see if Lady Stenhold is down?"

"She will be adequately entertained by Lord Blackmar."

"I am her companion," she reminded him.

A slender finger reached out to brush her jaw. In spite of herself, Bella felt a tingle of heat rush through her body.

"I have offered to make you mine."

With an effort, Bella ignored her traitorous reaction to his touch. "A most improper suggestion, my lord."

"Perhaps, but a delicious one, nonetheless."

"This is all so"—she allowed herself a breathless pause—"so sudden." Peeking from beneath her lashes, Bella watched his gaze narrow.

"Hardly sudden."

"A woman needs time to consider her feelings." She felt his body tense at her deliberate words.

"Indeed?"

"Oh, yes." She gave a toss of her head just as she had witnessed by countless other maidens. At the same moment she wondered if she appeared more like a mare with a bur beneath her saddle than a bewitching flirt. "I would never be with a gentleman for whom I did not care a great deal."

The wariness that had been simmering in his eyes deepened to a barely concealed alarm. "This is not about caring for each other," he cautiously back-tracked.

Bella was swift to press her advantage. "But, of course it is. How could it be otherwise?"

He took a step away, his brow furrowed together. "Mrs. Smith . . ."

"Yes, Philip?"

He carefully considered his words. For once his arrogance appeared to be in danger of slipping. "Are you attempting to imply that you have changed your mind?"

Slowly, Bella, she silently warned herself. She did not wish to startle him into a confession. Not until he had endured a sleepless night or two. "I was merely speaking my thoughts out loud," she coyly hedged. Then, as if on cue, the sound of the dinner bell resounded through the house. Bella heaved an inward sigh of relief. It was not an easy task to play to role of a tart. "Oh, we must go."

Lord Brasleigh opened his mouth as if to protest, but clearly realizing it would be rude to hold up dinner, he stiffly held out his arm to escort her to the dining room. She felt him studying her profile, but she kept her gaze firmly averted. Let him stew over her peculiar behavior. Perhaps it would sour his dinner.

They entered the dining room to discover that Lady Stenhold and Lord Blackmar were already seated at the long mahogany table. Lady Stenhold arched a silver brow as Lord Brasleigh escorted Bella to one of the gilt chairs and then took his own seat.

"There you are," she murmured. "I wondered if you would join us."

Bella struggled to maintain a cool composure beneath the older woman's scrutiny. Lady Stenhold was far too shrewd for comfort. "Lord Brasleigh was kindly helping me to choose a book."

"Oh?" Lady Stenhold turned her piercing gaze in Lord Brasleigh's direction. "And what did you select?"

Although Bella suspected that Lady Stenhold could detect a faint hint of color on his high cheekbones, Lord Brasleigh appeared as arrogantly in command as ever.

"We unfortunately were unable to decide among such a wealth of wonderful literature."

Although Lady Stenhold hesitated, as if debating whether or not to pursue their tardy entrance, she at last allowed herself to be distracted. "Oh, yes, Lord Stenhold was quite proud of his library."

"As he should be," Lord Brasleigh complimented. "I quite envy his collection."

"Are you a great reader, then?" Lady Stenhold inquired as the servants placed the turtle soup before them.

"I would not say great."

"Fah," Lord Blackmar abruptly intruded, his expression mocking. "Bras was always a tedious scholar. When the rest of us would slip from our rooms for a bit of a lark, he could be found in his room hunched over some tomb beside a flickering candle."

Bella could not halt her surprised glance toward Lord Brasleigh. A scholar? Surely a person had to possess a questing soul and sensitivity to find delight in the love for books?

Lord Brasleigh gave a faint shrug. "You make me sound quite dreary."

"I think it is quite commendable that you prefer

studies to Richard's notion of a lark," Lady Stenhold commented. "I recall they had him sent down
more than once. What do you think, Anna?"

Abruptly realizing that all eyes were upon her,
Bella hastily recalled her latest role. Not an easy
task. Ward. Widow. Flirt. It was difficult to recall
who she was to be at any given moment. The only
thing she truly wanted was to be free.

She turned to toss Lord Brasleigh a smile. "I
have always greatly admired scholars," she simpered.

Lord Brasleigh gave a sudden cough as his wine
became lodged in his throat. "You shall quite put
me to the blush," he managed to mutter.

Perhaps sensing the unease in the air, Lady Stenhold took command of the conversation. "Then
perhaps we should discuss the small gathering that
I intend to hold here at Mayfield."

"A gathering!" Lord Blackmar cried, a wicked
glint in his eyes. "What a delightful notion, eh,
Bras?"

"Delightful," Lord Brasleigh dutifully agreed, although there was a decided lack of enthusiasm in
his voice.

"It will be the perfect opportunity to introduce
you to the neighborhood," Lady Stenhold stated
firmly. "I will warn you that it shall be a most modest affair."

"No matter how modest, or how grand the event,
Mrs. Smith is bound to be the most beautiful lady
present, just as you, Aunt Caroline, shall be the
most elegant," Lord Blackmar proclaimed with lavish praise.

"Very pretty, Richard," Lady Stenhold retorted
with a knowing smile. "Perhaps I shall give you a

small token to hold you over until your next quarterly allowance, after all."

Lord Blackmar raised a dramatic hand to his heart. "I have always said that you are my dearest aunt."

Eight

Seated at the table, Philip glanced through the morning paper while his breakfast grew cold on his plate. Not that he actually read any of the various tidings from Brussels or the current rumors surrounding the prince. Instead, his thoughts brooded upon his restless night.

He did not like feeling as if a situation was slipping out of his control. He was a man who was always in command of himself and those around him. He was a leader, not some bufflehead who was content to be a victim of fate.

So why, then, did he feel as if he were suddenly sailing in decidedly treacherous waters?

An unknowing frown tugged at his dark brows. It had all begun with that blasted kiss. It had only been meant to frighten the stubborn brat. Certainly he had never intended it to be a kiss of passion. But there was something . . .

He abruptly shied away from the disturbing memories and instead moved to his latest troubles. Not that they were so different. They still centered upon one golden-haired minx.

What the devil was she up to?

He had been thoroughly caught off guard by her

peculiar behavior last evening. She had seemed so . . . well, flirtatious, he had to concede. Which was absurd. Since his arrival, she had wavered between fear and fury at his presence. Not once had she regarded him as anything more than a threat to her secret.

Then last night she had suddenly been laughing and batting her lashes like the veriest light skirt. It was disconcerting to say the least.

So he had lain awake most of the night, attempting to convince himself that he had merely overreacted. Perhaps she feared that her violent dislike was making him suspicious. Or she presumed that she could begin to relax her guard since he would soon have no reason to linger. Or perhaps she had simply been in a giddy temperament.

All reasonable explanations, but he could not thoroughly dismiss his lingering unease.

Rattling his paper, he attempted to concentrate on the news from the Continent. It was silly to fret over nothing. He had just managed to focus his thoughts on the words before his eyes when the door was slowly pushed open. His momentary peace was instantly shattered as the slender form of Bella Lowe entered the room.

As she had been the evening before, she was attired in a new gown. And as was her gown last evening, the soft primrose material was cut to reveal a most astonishing amount of white shoulders and deliciously enticing bosom. He felt a tingle of heat as his gaze instinctively studied the fascinating curves shown with such perfection.

Good lord, he thought as he guiltily jerked his gaze back to her tiny face, he would ensure that her trousseau was considerably more modest in design. Poor LeMont would discover himself trampled beneath a bevy of love-struck fools if she were to appear in London attired in such a gown.

Unfortunately, for the moment he was unable to command her to return to her room and change into one of her less revealing gowns. Even if it did make his role as the callous seducer a distinctly dangerous proposition.

Telling himself he was being a fool, Philip laid aside his newspaper to regard Bella with a charming smile. "You are up early, my dear."

With a shrug, she drifted toward the table and took a seat close to his own. "It is too lovely a day to lay abed."

"I suppose you have a dozen errands that need your immediate attention," he murmured, referring to her habit of darting away whenever he was near.

Surprisingly, she gave a firm shake of her head. "No, indeed. I thought I would spend the day at Mayfield."

Philip swiftly told himself that she was no doubt exhausted from her ceaseless travels throughout the countryside. There couldn't be a home within twenty miles that she had not visited on a dozen occasions over the past days.

"My luck appears to be improving." He poured her a cup of tea and then instinctively added the precise amount of sugar she preferred.

"What do you mean?"

"I mean that I rarely see more of you than a brief glimpse at a distance. To think that I will have the pleasure of your companionship for the entire day seems the height of good fortune."

Something flickered in her dark eyes before her head dropped to hide her expression. "You have more charm than is good for you, my lord."

"I thought we had agreed to Philip?"

"But the servants," she protested in low tones.

He reached across to grasp the slender hand lying in her lap. "Very well. Then let us go somewhere so that we can be alone, and you will feel free to call me Philip."

Expecting her to jerk her hand free, he was caught off guard as he felt her give a small tremor and peek at him from beneath impossibly long lashes.

"Alone?"

He unconsciously frowned. "Yes."

"Where could we possibly be alone?"

"We could take a picnic to the woods."

"That does sound romantic," she shocked him by saying with a bat of those lashes. "It has been a long time since I enjoyed a picnic."

Philip could not have been more shocked if she had stripped off her gown and danced naked on the table. The unease that had plagued him all night returned with a vengeance. "So you will go?"

A smile curved her full lips. "You appear surprised."

"Well, you must admit that you have offered little encouragement since my arrival."

"I was shocked by your bold advances," she informed him softly. "I am a lady, after all."

"And now?"

Her head slowly lifted. "And now I must admit I am somewhat intrigued. You are a most persuasive gentleman."

The flattering words did nothing to ease his growing dismay. Intrigued? That was the last thing he wished. "I thought I was no gentleman," he reminded her.

We'd Like to Invite You to Subscribe to Zebra's Regency Romance Book Club and Give You a Gift of 4 Free Books as Your Introduction! *(Worth $19.96!)*

If you're a Regency lover, imagine the joy of getting 4 FREE Zebra Regency Romances and then the chance to have these lovely stories delivered to your home each month at the lowest price available! Well, that's our offer to you and here's how you benefit by becoming a Regency Romance subscriber:

- 4 FREE Introductory Regency Romances are delivered to your doorstep
- 4 BRAND NEW Regencies are then delivered each month (usually before they're available in bookstores)
- Subscribers save almost $4.00 every month
- Home delivery is always FREE
- You also receive a FREE monthly newsletter, which features author profiles, discounts, subscriber benefits, book previews and more
- No risks or obligations...in other words, you can cancel whenever you wish with no questions asked

Join the thousands of readers who enjoy the savings and convenience offered to Regency Romance subscribers. After your initial introductory shipment, you receive 4 brand-new Zebra Regency Romances each month to examine for 10 days. Then, if you decide to keep the books, you'll pay the preferred subscriber's price of just $4.00 per title. That's only $16.00 for all 4 books and there's never an extra charge for shipping and handling.

It's a no-lose proposition, so return the FREE BOOK CERTIFICATE today!

Say Yes to 4 Free Books!
Complete and return the order card to receive this
$19.96 value, ABSOLUTELY FREE!

If the certificate is missing below, write to:
Regency Romance Book Club
P.O. Box 5214, Clifton, New Jersey 07015-5214
or call TOLL-FREE 1-888-345-BOOK
Visit our website at www.kensingtonbooks.com.

FREE BOOK CERTIFICATE

YES! Please rush me 4 Zebra Regency Romances without cost or obligation. I understand that each month thereafter I will be able to preview 4 brand-new Regency Romances FREE for 10 days. Then, if I should decide to keep them, I will pay the money-saving preferred subscriber's price of just $16.00 for all 4...that's a savings of almost $4 off the publisher's price with no additional charge for shipping and handling. I may return any shipment within 10 days and owe nothing, and I may cancel this subscription at any time. My 4 FREE books will be mine to keep in any case.

Name _____

Address _____ Apt. _____

City _____ State _____ Zip _____

Telephone ( ) _____

Signature _____
(If under 18, parent or guardian must sign.)   RN051A

Terms and prices subject to change. Orders subject to acceptance by Regency Romance Book Club.
Offer valid in U.S. only.

PLACE
STAMP
HERE

ll...l..lll....lll.l.l.l.l..l.l.l.l.l.l.l..ll.l..l

REGENCY ROMANCE BOOK CLUB
Zebra Home Subscription Service, Inc.
P.O. Box 5214
Clifton NJ 07015-5214

She gave a tiny giggle. "Shame on you, sir, for remembering my unkind words."

His gaze narrowed. "I could hardly forget them."

Pulling her hand free, she took a sip of her tea. "I must admit I was frightened."

"Of me?"

"I have never met anyone like you," she simpered.

"I assure you that the feeling is entirely mutual." His own tones were dry.

She clearly took his words as a compliment. "Oh, I fear I am quite common."

Philip couldn't halt the sharp laugh. He had met dozens and dozens of women. Some beautiful, some intelligent, and some blessed with a tangible charm. But never had he encountered a female who could keep his life in constant turmoil. "No, there is nothing common about you, Mrs. Smith," he assured her.

Again she gave that uncharacteristic giggle. "There, you see, you always know how to make a lady feel special. I suppose you are very experienced?"

A ridiculous heat crawled beneath his skin at the sudden question. "Experienced?"

"With women."

It was hardly a subject he wished to discuss with his ward. Or any innocent maiden for that matter. "No more so than any other gentleman of my advanced years," he retorted in repressive tones.

Her eyes widened. "I am sorry. Did I say something wrong?"

"I am not in the habit of discussing my private affairs."

She appeared to sense his discomfort. "I merely

meant that you seem very practiced at this sort of thing."

With an effort, Philip attempted to regain command of the situation. "Clearly not practiced enough," he said smoothly. "You have appeared remarkably immune."

She shrugged. "As I said, I was frightened."

"There is no need to be frightened."

She set aside her tea and leaned toward him, in the process, making him uncomfortably conscious of her indecent neckline. "No. I am beginning to realize that."

His heart skipped a sudden beat. "You are?"

"Yes, indeed." She leaned even closer. Blast. How was he to concentrate on her peculiar behavior when his vision was filled with such temptation? "I have tried to convince myself that it is wrong to succumb to your flirtations, but it is a battle I fear I am losing."

Desperately, he forced himself to forget the delectable curves and instead contemplate his brewing troubles. "Are you?"

"Yes."

"This is very sudden."

"Oh, no, not sudden at all," she protested, seemingly unable to recall her fierce dislike since his arrival. "I have realized since you came to Mayfield that you are a very attractive gentleman."

"I . . . see."

"Of course, I am not so shallow as to only consider a gentleman's countenance and fine form."

He was almost afraid to inquire further. "No?"

She gave a decisive shake of her head. "No. I have been very moved by your kindness to Miss Summers."

"I do not see why. She is very easy to be kind to."

"But no other gentleman has ever made the effort," Bella persisted. "She is quite changed since your arrival."

Philip inwardly cursed his instinctive sympathy for the vicar's daughter. He had never been able to resist the plight of those too weak or too frightened to defend themselves. And the sight of the timid Miss Summers being bullied by her beastly father had been tailored to tug at his heart. It had never occurred to him that his impulsive kindness would make an impression upon Bella. Now he realized he would have to nip any foolish fantasies in the bud.

"I hope, my dear, that you are not casting me in the role of the noble gentleman," he warned. "I fear that it really will not fit."

She appeared remarkably unaffected by his words. "You are far too modest, sir."

He gave a sudden snort. "I have never been accused of that before."

She pouted her lips in a manner that drew attention to their satin softness. A softness that he knew with intimate familiarity.

"Perhaps because you take such care to hide your kind heart."

He pulled away, determined to convince her that he was reprehensible beyond measure, only to be interrupted as Lady Stenhold entered the room attired in a moss-green morning gown.

"Good morning." She regarded her guests with a slow smile.

"Lady Stenhold." Philip rose to his feet and offered the older lady a chair. She gracefully took her seat in a cloud of rose fragrance.

"You two are up and about very early this morning."

"Lord Brasleigh has requested that I join him for a picnic this afternoon," Bella blurted out in bright tones.

Not surprisingly, Lady Stenhold turned her head to regard Philip with raised brows. "Has he?"

"Unless you need me to help with the arrangements for the ball?" Bella generously offered.

Lady Stenhold's gaze never wavered. "Certainly not. You go and enjoy yourself."

Bella rose to her feet. "I should arrange a basket with Cook."

With a grace that made her appear to float across the room, Bella moved to the door and into the hall. Left alone with Lady Stenhold, Philip was forced to meet that unnerving stare.

Lady Stenhold launched directly into battle. "Such a lovely young lady."

"Yes, indeed," Philip murmured, feeling decidedly uneasy.

"I have grown very fond of her. In truth, I have begun to think of her as my own daughter."

The warning was delivered with all the subtlety of a cannon ball, and being a wise veteran of battle, Philip was swift to form a strategic retreat. He was in no humor to cross swords with his hostess. "Excuse me. I must speak with Richard."

With a brief bow, Philip left the room and made his way determinedly through the hall and up the stairs. He barely hesitated as he came to Pudding's chamber and abruptly pushed open the door. He had to speak with someone about his deepening suspicions.

Entering the room, he discovered his friend propped upon a massive bed, partaking of a hearty breakfast. A faint smile touched his lips as he realized that even Lord Blackmar's dressing gown was a blinding canary hue.

Slowly turning his head, Pudding regarded his unexpected guest with a sardonic expression. "Good lord, Bras, it is devilishly early to be bursting your way into a gentleman's chambers."

"I need to speak with you," Philip retorted without apology.

Pudding heaved a sigh as he carefully wiped his mouth with a linen napkin and set aside the tray. "About Miss Lowe, no doubt."

Philip gave a startled frown. "How did you know?"

"Because she is all you have spoken of since we arrived."

Philip was taken aback. "Nonsense."

Pudding's lips twisted. "What has occurred?"

For a moment Philip debated whether to confess his troubled thoughts or not. It was clear his friend was in a teasing mood, and he had no desire to have such a delicate subject become a source of amusement. Still, he had to discuss his difficulties with someone, and Pudding appeared to be his only option.

Feeling ridiculously embarrassed, he shuffled his feet. "I believe Miss Lowe is beginning to . . ."

"Yes," Pudding prompted when Philip hesitated.

Philip hardened his features. "Develop feelings for me."

"Oh?"

"She acted very oddly yesterday and again this morning."

Pudding merely raised his brows. "What do you mean by oddly?"

With a restless motion, Philip paced across the carpet. He felt like a damn fool confessing his concerns. "Until yesterday she regarded me as if I were a particularly nasty plague she wished to be rid of with all possible speed. But suddenly . . . She is flirting like a practiced courtesan."

Pudding's brows rose even higher at Philip's words. "You don't say."

Reaching the white marble chimneypiece, Philip turned about to retrace his steps. "And now she has agreed to join me for a private picnic in the woods," he muttered, coming to an abrupt halt as Pudding's laughter suddenly echoed through the room. "Do you find that amusing?"

His icy tone only seemed to add to Pudding's humor. "Vastly amusing," he assured Philip.

"I fail to see why."

Lying back in his pillows, Pudding regarded Philip's dark expression with rather smug satisfaction. "I did warn you, if you will recall."

"Warn me? About what, pray?"

"For goodness' sakes, you have done everything possible to seduce a young maiden who hasn't the least experience with a gentleman. How could she possibly not tumble into love with you?"

Love? Philip instantly stiffened at the absurd notion. Clearly Pudding knew nothing about the fairer sex if he believed they could be won by a few outrageous propositions from an out-and-out bounder.

"You are spouting a lot of nonsense. I made it very clear that my intentions were grossly dishonorable."

Pudding waved aside his words. "But she is a fanciful chit. She only sees a handsome lord offering her the type of attention she has never before received."

Philip couldn't deny the truth in Pudding's accusation. Good heavens, he had never considered the notion that Bella had indeed been sheltered for most of her life. How many gentlemen could she possibly have encountered? Not more than a handful, he would wager, and precious few her own age. What a buffoon he had been not to have taken her innocence into account sooner.

Without warning, the memory of her trembling form pressed to his own rose to his mind. Had he been the first to kiss those satin lips? The first to hear those soft moans from deep in her throat?

The stirring warmth in his thighs abruptly recalled Philip to the present. Blast. Why had he ever kissed her in the first place? It had caused nothing but trouble ever since.

"This is a bloody mess," he muttered.

"What will you do?"

Philip clenched his hands in tight fists. There might have been a few unexpected difficulties in his battle to marry off Miss Lowe, but that did nothing more than strengthen his determination to haul her to the alter.

"Clearly, I must prove that I am wholly and utterly unworthy of affection," he retorted, heaving an exasperated sigh as Pudding once again burst out in merry laughter. "Would you please halt that?"

Thoroughly unrepentant, Pudding lifted his hands. "It is so deliciously ironic, old boy. I am beginning to be quite pleased that I agreed to this delightful trip to Surrey. It is more entertaining than any farce on the stages of London."

Philip slapped his hands to his hips. So Pudding found his troubles entertaining? He enjoyed a good farce? Well, Philip would be only too happy to oblige.

Moving toward the bed, he plucked the waiting

pitcher of water off the side table and poured the entire contents over the head of his chuckling friend.

Nine

It was a perfect day for a picnic. The unpredictable spring weather had offered up a hint of summer with a clear blue sky and a warm breeze that carried the sweet scent of wildflowers. Not that Bella paid much heed to the lovely weather. She was far more intent on the large male that walked silently at her side.

Since he had joined her in the foyer and taken charge of the large basket of food, he had appeared remarkably distracted. A good sign, she firmly told herself. He was clearly beginning to fear that his ploy was going terribly wrong.

Of course, her satisfaction was somewhat tempered by her own inner unease. As difficult as it might be to accept, she could not completely deny that she possessed a most absurd awareness of Lord Brasleigh as a man. She might wish to blame her tremors and tingles on anger, or fear of discovery. But even with her undoubted innocence, she could not deny that Lord Brasleigh had only to brush her arm or touch her cheek and her entire body flared with a heady heat. Even her sleep was beginning to be haunted by the most unmaidenly dreams.

And why not? she sternly chastised herself. Lord

Brasleigh was without a doubt an extraordinarily handsome gentleman. With his elegant features, raven hair, and silver eyes, he quite put any other gentlemen in the shade. And as for his lean, muscular form . . .

She abruptly drew her mind away from such dangerous thoughts. Granted, she was female enough to react to a handsome gentleman, but that in no way changed the fact that he had ruthlessly attempted to manipulate her into marriage, or that he considered her a meaningless burden that was to be dispensed with the least bother to himself.

Unfortunately, her impetuous decision to punish him for his treachery meant that she would have to openly encourage his caresses. She would have to ensure that she did not allow her absurd reactions to distract her from the task at hand.

Drawing in a deep breath, Bella steeled her courage to continue her charade. "Is it much further?"

His dark head suddenly turned so he could regard her with a searching gaze. "Are you nervous?"

"Not at all," she promptly lied with a sweet smile. "My feet are merely tired."

The dark eyes flickered at her breezy retort. "There is a small opening just ahead. It will allow us all the privacy we desire."

Perfect for her plans, she acknowledged as she squashed the renegade flare of unease. Perfect. "How nice."

Stepping ahead of Bella, Lord Brasleigh pushed aside the thick bushes to reveal a small glade complete with a tiny stream. "Here we are," he announced, taking Bella's hand and pulling her into the opening. She stood to one side as he competently spread out the blanket and then began unloading the basket of goodies. Pheasants, meat pies, potatoes in cream sauce, and tarts were spread across the blanket. Then, retrieving a bottle and two glasses from the bottom of the basket, he regarded her with a slow smile. "Champagne?"

"Thank you," she murmured as he handed her a glass of the bubbling liquid.

Lifting his own glass, he allowed his gaze to drift over her with appreciation. "You look very beautiful."

She felt as if there was not a nook or cranny of her form that he had not inspected. Still, she managed what she hoped was a seductive smile. "Do you think so?"

He deliberately scooted closer. "So beautiful that I wish to see more of you."

Bella caught her breath. Not yet. She was not prepared to play her winning card. "Should we not eat?"

He leaned forward until his breath sweetly brushed her cheek. "I am not hungry for food."

Her heart skipped a beat. "Cook will be very disappointed if we do not at least sample her delicacies."

"If you insist." He slowly pulled back.

To cover the awkward moment, Bella reached for the plates and filled them with the tempting food. Then, handing the silent Lord Brasleigh his plate, she settled back and desperately searched for a means of prolonging the inevitable.

She at last hit upon a topic. "Tell me of Italy."

A hint of satisfaction shimmered in his silver eyes, as if he were pleased by her obvious tactics. "What do you wish to know?"

"Is it lovely?"

"Very lovely," he answered swiftly, his expression softening. "I walked the roads of Nero, stood in the shadows of the Coliseum, and gazed in wonder at the ceiling of the Sistine Chapel."

Bella found herself intrigued in spite of herself. She had always wished she could travel throughout the continent. And Italy would have been one of her favorite places to visit. The art, the music, the sweeping history that was as grand as time itself. "Did you see the *Pietà?*" she demanded, referring to Michealangelo's famous statue.

"Yes." His voice took on a husky note of sincerity. "It was the most powerful, moving piece of art that I have ever had the fortune to gaze upon. It is impossible to believe it was ever a chunk of marble."

Bella briefly forgot her role, and even the fact she was furious with this gentleman. She had read so much of the fabulous treasures in Italy, she was anxious to hear them described firsthand. "How wonderful. I can think of nothing I should enjoy more than to wander among such famous works."

He gave a sudden grimace. "Of course, many of the treasures were stolen by Napoleon when he imposed his Treaty of Tolentino. It was said that he used more than five hundred wagons to carry his bounty from the Vatican to Paris. It is to be hoped they will be returned now that the Corsican monster has been exiled."

"It is an outrage."

"Of course, Napoleon could not steal the essence of Italy." His smile returned.

"The essence?"

He reached out to refill her glass with champagne. "The smell, the food . . . the people. Never have I met such warm and open souls."

Bella felt a pang of envy. How she would love to be free to travel the world. "They sound fascinating."

"We even encountered a band of gypsies."

Her eyes widened. "Really?"

"My companions, Wickton, Challmond, and I were out riding one day when we saved an old woman from some local scoundrels. As a reward we were given a special blessing."

"What was that?"

"A love that is true, a heart that is steady, a wounded soul healed, a spirit made ready. Three women will come, as the seasons will turn, and bring true love to each, before the summer again burns . . ." he softly quoted.

Bella's temporary sense of ease with this man was abruptly dispelled. She might be fascinated with his travels through Italy, but she had no interest in his true love. Indeed, the mere thought was enough to make her heart give an odd twinge. "Very pretty," she forced herself to utter. "Do you believe it?"

His lips twisted. "True love? I prefer my relationships less complicated."

She did not doubt that for a moment. A gentleman spoiled by wealth and adulation would have no need for the security of love and a family.

Unlike herself . . .

"Who are Wickton and Challmond?" she demanded.

A genuine smile lit his features. "Two of my dearest friends. They helped me to keep my sanity during the war. Not an easy task when you are surrounded by chaos."

"Do they believe in the blessing?"

Lord Brasleigh gave a short laugh. "Wickton is unfortunately in a position where he must wed for a dowry rather than love, and Challmond is far too wily to be caught in the tantalizing web of a woman."

They sounded as arrogant and unfeeling as Lord

Brasleigh. "How cynical you are, my lord," she said lightly.

His gaze once again drifted over her slender form. "There is no one here, my dear. You have promised to call me Philip."

She hesitated and then realized that she could delay no longer. She had come on this picnic to make Lord Brasleigh rue his presence at Mayfield, and it was time she began. Praying that she did not lose her nerve, she smiled slowly.

"Very well . . . Philip."

Setting aside his plate, he leaned closer. "I like the sound of my name upon your lips."

"It is a very good name." She pretended to consider her words. "Strong and persuasive, just like you."

There was a moment's pause before he reached for her untouched plate and empty glass.

"I believe we can dispense with this," he murmured.

"Yes." With the champagne going straight to her head, Bella felt a surge of bold confidence rush through her. Slowly lifting her arms, she began removing the pins from her hair. She heard Lord Brasleigh's breath catch as the golden curls tumbled about her shoulders.

"What are you doing?" Lord Brasleigh demanded.

"You said that you liked my hair."

An indefinable expression rippled over his handsome features as his hand rose of its own accord to stroke the satin tresses. "It is like silk," he breathed.

She stoically ignored the warmth of his hand and the scent of his male skin. "I have never had a gentleman tell me such things. It has quite turned my head."

His eyes were the color of smoke. "I only speak the truth."

"But in such a charming manner."

As if abruptly coming to his senses, Lord Brasleigh dropped his hand. "Charming?"

"Certainly you are charming," she cooed. "And so handsome."

Pulling back, Lord Brasleigh regarded her with a faint frown. "Mrs. Smith . . ."

"Yes?"

"I hope that you have not misunderstood my intentions."

She forced her eyes wide. "What do you mean?"

"My stay in Surrey will be very brief," he retorted bluntly.

Ha. His stay is already far too long, she seethed. She cursed the day he had ever arrived at Mayfield. Somehow she kept her smile intact. "And then you will return to London?"

His expression was guarded. "Yes."

Bella heaved a deep sigh. "I have always wished to see London."

It was not at all what he had expected. "What?"

"You did promise me an establishment, did you not?" she demanded.

He could not disguise his shock at her words. Bella felt a flare of satisfaction.

"You are willing to become my mistress?" he demanded, his tone sounding as if he would have more easily believed she was willing to join the French army.

"You have not changed your mind, have you?"

"It is not that, but . . . I do not believe that you have given this the proper thought."

Bella prepared to deliver her most potent weapon.

"How can a woman think properly when she is in love?"

He jerked backward as if he had been burned. It was difficult for Bella not to laugh at the comical expression of horror on his handsome countenance.

"I have warned you that this has nothing to do with love," he said harshly.

Her lashes fluttered. "Perhaps not for you."

He shook his head as if he could still not believe she was in earnest. Bella's satisfaction deepened. She knew precisely how he was feeling. Had she not been wracked with fear and disbelief for days? It seemed utterly fitting.

"I do not want any complications."

She shrugged. "You have made that very clear."

His lips thinned. She could almost hear his thoughts churning with the fierce dilemma of whether to confess the truth and end the charade or continue in the hopes of frightening her into obeying his commands.

"My intentions do not include marriage."

At least not for him, she acknowledged. It was one thing to force his ward into wedlock and quite another to take the unwelcome step himself. "That suits me well enough," she retorted in firm tones.

Bella heard his breath hiss between his teeth.

"Is that so?"

"Oh, yes." She offered what she hoped was a provocative smile. "I fear my . . . experience with gentlemen has convinced me never to place myself within their care. I prefer to control my own future."

His features hardened at her explanation. "And you believe you can do that as my mistress?"

She shuddered at the mere thought. Although he

was no doubt a master in the art of seduction—her own reluctant reaction to him was proof of that— she was quite certain that he would always be in stern control of the relationship and his own emotions. Unlike her, he was not an impetuous, deeply emotional sort. Unless, of course, one had managed to pierce his armor and enter his heart, a renegade voice murmured in the back of her mind. Clearly, he was fiercely loyal and dedicated to his mother and friends.

She shoved her nonsensical thoughts aside. It was nothing to her how he might treat his loved ones or his lovers. Her only concern was how despicably he treated his ward.

"My life will be my own as your mistress. Something that would never occur as your wife."

A muscle twitched in his jaw as he realized that he could not argue with her logic. "And when I tire of you?"

She refused to be daunted. How delightful it was to see him struggle with his rising panic. "Then I shall no longer be your concern."

A silence fell at her simple words. In the distance, the sound of chirping birds could be heard, and closer the occasional rustle of a small animal in the underbrush.

It was clear that Lord Brasleigh noted none of this as he slowly shook his head. "It appears that you have quite made up your mind."

"I fear that you have changed yours," she challenged.

His mouth thinned as he decided to give his ploy one last desperate try. "I just wished to be assured there were no misunderstandings. It can make it very awkward when I choose a new mistress."

With a very deliberate motion, Bella leaned forward. "Perhaps you will never wish to possess another mistress."

His gaze lowered to her full lips before abruptly being wrenched back to her wide eyes. "That is hardly likely."

Now was the moment, and Bella discovered herself absurdly grateful that the champagne still flowed through her veins. It would take every ounce of her courage to finish her revenge.

Scooting forward, she lifted a hand to cup his cheek. "I will make you very happy."

She felt the tremor of shock race through his body at her bold touch. "No doubt . . ." His voice came to a choked halt as her fingers drifted over his firm lips. "Mrs. Smith."

"Yes?" she murmured.

His hands lifted to grasp her roaming fingers. "Please stop."

In response, Bella scooted even closer, her soft frame pressed to his side. "Have I done something wrong?"

He sucked in an audible breath, his hand clenching her fingers in a painful grip. "No, there is something I must tell you."

"You can tell me later." With more daring that she would ever have thought she possessed, she moved until her lips pressed the line of his jaw. A blaze of heat flared through her body at the intimate contact, and she was deeply relieved when he pulled away sharply.

It was indecent that a gentleman she did not even like should make her heart pound and her stomach quiver in such a fashion.

"No." His voice was barely recognizable.

She pretended to be hurt at his rejection. "But, my lord, this is what you wished."

"No, it is not."

"But . . ." Determined to force him to confess his treachery, Bella was compelled to curb her impatience as the unmistakable sound of hurried footsteps echoed through the trees. "Someone is coming."

With none of his usual grace, Lord Brasleigh thrust himself to his feet. Far more slowly, Bella rose as well.

Within moments a young footman pushed his way into the clearing. "My lord, Lady Stenhold asked me to find you."

"Has something occurred?" Lord Brasleigh demanded.

"You have guests at Mayfield who wish to see you."

"Guests? Who are they?"

"I fear I do not know, my lord."

Lord Brasleigh slanted a mystified glance toward Bella before returning his attention to the servant. "We shall be there in a moment."

The footman gave a bow. "Very good, my lord."

Waiting until they were once again alone, Lord Brasleigh turned to regard her with a set expression. "We must go," he reluctantly conceded. "But I have need to speak with you as soon as possible."

She allowed a slow smile to curve her lips. "But, of course, my lord. I eagerly await our conversation."

Ten

Feeling a flare of exasperation at the intrusion, Philip efficiently packed away the remains of the picnic and folded the blanket. At his side, he was disturbingly aware of Bella as she gathered her golden curls and pulled them back into a tidy knot.

A tremor shook his body. Heaven above, his blood had turned to flames when those curls had tumbled about her bare shoulders. He wanted to forget that she was his ward, that she was as innocent as a babe, and that he would soon be handing her to Monsieur LeMont. He wished only to pull her into his arms and rid himself of the growing ache that kept him awake during the long nights.

The image of her laid upon the blanket while he . . .

No. Abruptly shaking his head, he thrust the reprehensible thoughts away.

It was time for the game to end. Past time, he acknowledged as he recalled the maiden's fervent desire to become his mistress.

It had clearly been an absurd notion to begin with. Nothing had gone as it should. Bella was no closer to accepting her marriage to Monsieur

LeMont. And he . . . He was behaving as if he had never before encountered an attractive female.

He should have remained in London and forgotten he had ever possessed a bloody ward. At least then he would not be plagued by his strangely unpredictable emotions.

Holding aside the branches, Philip waited for Bella to step onto the path before joining her. Then, with a great deal of reluctance, he held out his arm and escorted her back toward the house. He gave little thought to his mysterious guests. Instead, he brooded upon the best means of informing Miss Lowe that, far from desiring an affair with a young widow, he knew precisely who she was and had merely plotted to frighten her into marriage.

She would be furious, of course. Not only would she be embarrassed by her shocking lack of modesty, but she was about to discover her absurd flight had not saved her from his control.

Oh, yes, she would be furious indeed.

In silence, they left the woods and crossed the scythed lawn to enter the house. With a sideways glance, Miss Lowe at last spoke. "Were you expecting guests, my lord?"

"Not at all." He handed the basket and blanket to a hovering footman. His hat and gloves he placed on a side table. "I know very few people in the area."

"Perhaps it is someone who is simply traveling through Surrey."

"Perhaps." He did not care who it might be, as long as they possessed the sense to keep the visit brief.

They had taken only a few steps down the hallway when the door to the drawing room was pulled open and Lady Stenhold moved to greet them. "There you are, my lord."

"Lady Stenhold."

"I apologize for intruding upon your picnic, but I thought you would like to know that you have visitors."

"Of course."

With a nod, Lady Stenhold turned to head further along the hallway, clearly allowing him a measure of privacy with his callers.

Keeping Bella at his side, Philip entered the room. Just for a moment, he regarded the large, horse-faced matron and the slender, dark-haired gentleman seated upon the sofa with a flare of annoyance. They were clearly of the mushroom variety, who believed that they could be introduced to a gentleman and then promptly claim friendship with him. In London, he was besieged by such vulgar upstarts, but he had not expected to be harassed in such a remote location. Then, as the young man slowly rose to his feet, Philip felt as if he had been slugged in the stomach.

Good gads! Madam LeMont and her son Andre. How could they possibly be here? He had left them in London to await his return. He certainly had not revealed where he was going. And now he was in a true muddle.

Good lord, could the day get any worse?

Seemingly undisturbed by the fact that she had intruded upon a private gathering, Madam LeMont smiled in a smug fashion. "My dear Lord Brasleigh," she gushed, her broad frame hideously encased in a puce gown with a profusion of ribbons. "How utterly wonderful to see you again."

A fine shiver of distaste raced through his body even as he gave a stiff bow. "Madam LeMont."

The woman gave a grating laugh. "We have surprised you, have we not?"

His lips twisted. Surprise was not precisely the word he would have used. "Yes."

Clearly more perceptive than his mother, Andre sensed Philip's lack of enthusiasm. A slender young man with delicate features and large brown eyes, he possessed a sensitivity that was overtly lacking in his mother.

"I warned you, Mother, that we should not simply descend upon his lordship," he said in low tones.

"Nonsense." Madam LeMont waved a pudgy hand. "Lord Brasleigh is almost family. Surely there is no need to stand upon ceremony. Is there, my lord?"

Directly confronted, Philip could hardly claim that she was as welcome as the plague. Still . . . almost family? What a ghastly notion. "Of course not," he lied smoothly. "But I did not realize that you intended to visit Surrey."

"London was terribly flat without you, and when we learned that you had traveled to the country, we decided to follow."

Philip was not deceived. He had no doubt the greedy woman had followed him out of fear he might change his mind and offer his generous dowry to another. "I see."

"Of course, we hoped that you would have brought your lovely ward along with you." She came directly to the point. "Andre is most anxious to meet her."

Philip grimaced. The moment had come, and he could only shudder at the thought of Bella's reaction. "Oh . . . yes."

Andre shifted his feet in embarrassment. "Mother,

I really believe it would be best if we went to the inn and returned to London in the morning."

His suggestion was rewarded by an impatient glare from his mother. "Andre, please allow me to handle the situation. I cannot imagine Lord Brasleigh would wish us to hurry away when we have just arrived."

They couldn't hurry away fast enough as far as Philip was concerned, but he could only smile thinly. "Certainly not."

Madam LeMont smiled in a triumphant manner. "There, you see?"

"Of course, I am merely a guest of Lady Stenhold's," he was swift to point out.

"Lady Stenhold has already kindly issued a most generous invitation to remain at Mayfield as long as we wish," Madam LeMont said, squashing his faint hope. "Such a lovely lady."

"Yes, she is," Philip agreed, although he was not so kindly disposed toward his hostess at the moment.

"But we have not yet met your companion." Madam LeMont glanced pointedly toward the silent Bella.

Wishing himself back on Napoleon's battlefield, Philip turned toward the maiden at his side. "Forgive me. May I introduce my ward, Miss Lowe? Bella, this is Madam LeMont and her son, Monsieur LeMont."

Expecting stunned disbelief at the realization that he knew precisely who she was, Philip was baffled as Bella smiled with an icy composure. "How do you do?"

Predictably unaware of the tension in the air, Madam LeMont glanced toward her son. "There, did I not assure you that she would be charming, Andre?"

"She is, indeed." An engaging smile lit his thin face as Andre moved to raise Bella's fingers to his lips. "It is a delight, Miss Lowe."

"Thank you," Bella retorted in meek tones.

Philip's disbelief only deepened. She was behaving as if nothing on earth was amiss. She was even allowing her hand to remain in the clinging grasp of that . . . overly forward puppy.

Blast! Nothing appeared to make sense.

"Such a charming couple, do you not think, my lord?" Madam LeMont said in coy tones.

"Yes," Philip agreed abruptly, although he did not particularly care for Andre's lingering touch. For goodness' sakes, they had just met.

"I must warn you, my lord, that Andre has become a great favorite among the ladies," the older woman informed him.

"Has he?"

"Mother," Andre protested as he at last stepped from Bella.

"Oh, yes. There was more than one tear shed when it was learned that he would soon wed."

A hint of color washed Andre's countenance. "Miss Lowe cannot be interested in such absurd nonsense."

"I merely wished her to realize what a fortunate young maiden she is."

"She should be allowed to be the judge of that," Andre said stiffly.

Madam LeMont gave another grating laugh. "You are always so modest. Lord Brasleigh obviously considered you a most distinguished gentleman. Why else would he have chosen you for his ward?"

"Oh, yes," Bella suddenly spoke, casting a daggerlike glance toward Philip. "Lord Brasleigh has always been quite conscientious in his concern for me. He would do whatever necessary to ensure my happiness."

Her thrust hit home, and Philip took an impetuous step in her direction. "Bella."

"Yes . . . my lord?"

"Could I have a moment alone with you?"

She arched a golden brow. "And leave your guests?"

"I am certain they will excuse us for a moment."

She gave an indifferent shrug. "Perhaps later. I really should change for dinner." She turned to favor Andre with a sweet smile. "Excuse me."

Sweeping from the room, she ignored his outstretched hand. Philip was not to be put off so easily. Disregarding his ill manners, he muttered a low apology and charged in her wake.

He wanted to know precisely what the unruly chit was thinking, and more precisely what she intended to do. He had no desire to wake in the morning and discover that she had taken flight in the middle of the night.

As swift as he had been, he still did not manage to catch Bella until she was entering her chamber. Without regard to propriety, he followed behind her and firmly closed the door. "Bella."

She turned abruptly, her dark eyes blazing. "Yes, my lord?"

"I must speak with you."

"I said we could speak later."

His expression hardened. "Now."

Her hands clenched at her sides. "Is it not enough that you bully and threaten me, my lord? Must you also invade my very privacy?"

He refused to be swayed. "It appears that our game is at an end."

"It most certainly is."

He studied her set features. "You appear remarkably calm."

"Would you prefer that I toss a few of these lovely figurines at your arrogant head?" she demanded. "Believe me, few things would give me more pleasure."

He did not doubt for a moment that she would love to decorate his head with the fragile ornaments. "I realize you must be embarrassed—" he said, attempting to sympathize, only to be halted as she took a sharp step forward.

"Embarrassed? Why in heaven's name would I be embarrassed? You are the one who has behaved in a shameful manner."

A faint heat touched his cheekbones. Why, the annoying brat. Trust her to somehow blame him for the fiasco. "Perhaps you have forgotten what occurred between us in the woods this afternoon, but I assure you that I have not," he said in stiff tones.

Far from being humiliated at the reminder of her disreputable behavior, she merely smiled. "Certainly I have not forgotten. It went precisely according to my plan."

Philip slowly froze. "Plan?"

"My plan to teach you a well-deserved lesson in treating me as a fool," she informed him in cold tones. "I am well aware that you came to Mayfield to frighten me into marriage."

There was a shattering pause before Philip was giving a disbelieving shake of his head. "How could you know?"

"You are not nearly so clever as you believe, my lord."

Obviously not, he acknowledged, as he struggled to accept what she was saying. She had known that he never believed her to be a widow. All her claims of wishing to be his mistress were no more than a charade. It seemed impossible. Absurd.

"Lord Blackmar would not have told you," he muttered.

"It hardly matters how I know."

"No," he agreed, his lips thinning at the realization that he was the one who had been duped. A most uncommon occurrence. Indeed, he could not recall it ever happening before. "Nor does it excuse your behavior."

Her eyes widened in fury. "You, sir . . ." Words failed her for a brief moment. "My behavior is above reproach in comparison to your own."

"Above reproach?" He gave a sharp laugh. "You must have taken leave of your senses. Never in all my life have I encountered a lady who is so lacking in maidenly sensibilities and modesty."

She glared at him with open distaste. "And you have known many ladies, have you not, my lord?"

Damn the brat, he seethed. Her tongue was as sharp as a saber. "We are not discussing me, Miss Lowe. We are discussing you and your determination to behave as an unruly hoyden."

Her hands landed upon her hips in an aggressive stance. "Why? Because I did not wish to be hauled down the aisle and married off to a complete stranger?"

"Because you have been intolerable from the moment you became my ward," he snapped, goaded beyond all bearing. "I was perfectly content to allow you to remain at my estate with a suitable companion, but you proved that you could not be trusted. Not only did you make my entire staff miserable with your unforgivable behavior, but you managed to run off every decent companion I could find."

"Companions?" She gave a laugh of her own. "Did you ever once personally meet my delightful companions?"

He ignored the tiny prick of guilt. He had more than done his duty to this impossible woman. "I could hardly be expected to personally interview every staff member," he informed her in lofty tones. "I did, however, ensure that each and every one had impeccable references."

Her expression was mocking. "Oh, yes, why should you be bothered to actually meet with the women I was forced to live with day after day?"

He drew in a deep breath, ignoring the faint scent of lavender in the air. He did not need the distraction of realizing they were very much alone in her chamber. Or that within a few steps he could have her off her feet and onto the wide bed. "They were all highly recommended."

"Perhaps they were, but I assure you they were impossible to endure."

"Why? Because they expected you to behave in a manner befitting a young maiden?"

"Because they were incompetent fools."

He regarded her with scathing disbelief. "Absurd."

Bella's tiny face flushed with a dark heat at his implication that she was not being entirely truthful. Raising her hand she held up one finger. "The first supposed companion was a mean-spirited dragon who threatened to have my puppies drowned in the lake." She lifted a second finger. "The next proved to possess a violent *tendre* for the local vicar and eventually fled when he chose to marry a maiden younger than myself." Another finger rose. "The next was caught attempting to steal my pearl necklace, followed by two more who detested the country and ensured I received the force of their ill humor, and the last was far too fond of sampling the fine cellar you possess, my lord." Her hand dropped, and she regarded him with a narrowed glare. "I can hardly be held at fault if you chose to hire lovelorn spinsters, thieves, and drunks."

Philip discovered himself taken aback by the vehemence in her tone. Was it possible that the chaperons his secretary had hired had proven to be so utterly undesirable? Granted, the women forced into such a position must have found it a demeaning proposition. And being in charge of such a high-spirited, beautiful young maiden could not be easy. Still . . . To think that they all had behaved in such a shocking fashion seemed difficult to accept. "You must be exaggerating."

Her glare did not waver. "I assure you that I am not."

Philip was at a dead-end. He could hardly prove that the women hadn't been thoroughly unreliable, and Bella was quite aware of the fact. Clearly, it was time for a strategic change of tactics. "That still does not excuse your flight from my protection nor your outrageous lies to Lady Stenhold."

Her impossibly long lashes fluttered at his direct hit. Since his arrival he had discovered that Bella was genuinely fond of Lady Stenhold and no doubt disliked lying to the older woman. He had used her affection deliberately.

"I will admit that I regret my pretense to Lady

Stenhold," she admitted stiffly. "But you left me no option."

His expression became one of disbelief. "You blame me?"

"Of course," she retorted without the slightest hesitation. "You are the one attempting to force me into marriage."

Philip decided that she had to be the most exasperating, unreasonable chit in all of England. "I am merely attempting to fulfill your father's wishes."

"And what about my wishes?"

"I believe Monsieur LeMont will make you a fine husband."

"I do not wish a husband."

"No," he growled in frustration. "You wish to be a shocking hellion, sneaking about the countryside, lying to susceptible widows, and exposing us both to scandal."

Fury rippled over Bella's tiny countenance. "Oh, yes, you are so concerned with scandal, are you not, my lord?"

Philip stiffened. "What does that mean?"

"You did not mind scandal when you paraded your actress about London and scorned every eligible debutante."

"That is none of your concern," he rasped in embarrassment. *Blast the chit.*

"Then what of your attempt to seduce your own ward?"

For a moment Philip was beyond words. How dare she imply he was so lacking in morals? He had never seduced an innocent in his life, let alone his ward. He far preferred sophisticated Cyprians.

He refused to admit that a portion of his anger might be caused by the undeniable heat that raced through his body whenever she was near, or the potent dreams that plagued his nights. That was something he was not yet prepared to consider.

"That was merely a means of ensuring you realized the dangers of your ridiculous behavior," he forced out between gritted teeth.

"Well, it did not succeed. The only thing that you have proven is that I will never entrust my life to the care of treacherous men."

It was suddenly all too much for Philip. He had followed Bella to make sure that she would behave in a reasonable manner in front of their guests, only to be accused of every sin known to man. Well, she could blame him all she liked, but she would obey him.

"What you will or will not do is entirely up to me, Miss Lowe. Do not forget that pertinent fact again." His warning delivered, he turned and stormed from the room, not at all surprised when the crash of a porcelain figurine followed in his wake.

Eleven

Bella watched with murder in her heart as Lord Brasleigh marched from the room. There was no one who could ruffle her temper with such ease. Or make her behave in a manner that would no doubt shame her mother. And at the same moment, she was humiliatingly aware of the scent of his warm skin and the lean strength of his body.

It was all so . . . maddening.

He refused to admit that he had behaved in a shameful manner. Or even that he was wrong to force her into a loveless marriage. In all his glorious arrogance, he simply presumed that his every decision was utterly perfect. Like a command from God Himself.

And then he had the audacity to behave as if this entire mess were entirely her fault.

Her fault?

With jerky movements she struggled to remove her gown. As furious as she might be with Lord Brasleigh, her concern should be with finding Lady Stenhold and somehow confessing her secret. The unexpected arrival of Madam LeMont and her son meant that her identity could no longer be kept a secret. She did not want the dear lady to discover the truth from anyone but herself.

Tossing aside her gown, she thankfully reached for one of her own far more modest dresses. She chose a pale lilac satin with a simple ivory lace over-skirt. She pulled her hair atop her head and allowed a sprinkling of curls to nuzzle her cheeks and the curve of her neck. Lastly, she clasped on her mother's pearls.

Ready as she would ever be, she left her rooms and hurried down the hall to Lady Stenhold's chambers. After a brief tap, she entered slowly to discover the older woman seated in front of the cheval looking glass.

The main chamber was a vast room designed in a French empire style. Ivory panels with an abundance of gilded moldings were offset with French ebony furnishings. A boulle armoire was placed along one wall, a canopy bed dominated the center of the room, and a delicate Mazarin desk was tucked in a distant corner. It was a room that perfectly matched Lady Stenhold. Elegant and yet sprinkled with just a hint of whimsy.

At her entrance, the older woman shifted to regard her with a faint smile. "Hello, my dear."

"Forgive me for intruding."

"Not at all." Lady Stenhold waved a hand to a gilt-and-ebony chair. "Please have a seat."

"Thank you." Bella perched on the edge of the cushion.

She felt a decided pang of reluctance at the thought of disappointing the woman who had come to mean a great deal in her life. Lady Stenhold was the first person who had opened her home to her out of friendship rather than duty or money. Bella wished that she did not have to ruin their budding relationship.

"I trust that Lord Brasleigh has added his invitation to my own for his guests to remain at Mayfield?"

Although Bella had been shocked by the unexpected arrival of the LeMonts, she was in enough possession of her faculties to recall a poetically handsome young gentleman with soft brown eyes and a large woman with a loud voice and unpleasantly forceful manner. Trust Lord Brasleigh to choose a gentleman with a mother that would make her life a misery, she inwardly seethed.

"I do not believe Madam LeMont is in need of a second invitation," she said in wry tones. "She appears determined to stay as long as necessary."

Lady Stenhold regarded her with mild curiosity. "Are you acquainted with Madam LeMont?"

"No," Bella automatically denied, then swiftly checked herself. It was time the lies came to an end. "That is . . ."

"Yes?"

Bella's gaze dropped to where her hands had twisted into knots in her lap. "This is very difficult."

"Is something the matter?" Lady Stenhold probed gently.

Bella drew in a deep breath. This was every bit as horrible as she had expected. "Actually, I have a confession to make," she admitted in strained tones.

"Oh, my, that sounds ominous." Lady Stenhold did not appear particularly concerned. Indeed, a hint of amusement could be detected deep in her eyes. "Should I pour us a brandy?"

Bella could not prevent a wry smile. Somehow

this woman always managed to make her feel as if everything was going to be just fine. "We shall no doubt have need of it later."

"It cannot be that bad."

"I fear that it is." Bella steeled her quavering nerves and prepared for Lady Stenhold's anger. "You see, I am not Anna Smith."

Bella unconsciously held her breath as she waited for Lady Stenhold's outraged disbelief at her treachery. After all, the woman had opened her home to Bella with the belief that she was a poor widow with no resources and no family. The realization that she was harboring a liar and a runaway was bound to make her feel betrayed.

Shockingly, however, the older woman merely regarded her with a faint smile. Almost as if she were not surprised at all. Bella could only presume she did not fully comprehend the situation.

"Are you not?"

"No," she said in firm tones. "My name is Miss Bella Lowe."

"Miss Lowe," Lady Stenhold repeated the name, an odd expression of satisfaction settling on her countenance. "Lord Brasleigh's ward."

Bella was decidedly confused. The woman was not behaving at all as she had expected. Why was she not furious—or at least shocked by her confession? She sat there as if her houseguests pretended to be someone else every day.

"Yes, I am."

"I suppose that also means that you were not married to poor Lieutenant Smith?"

Bella flushed at the memory of Lady Stenhold's concern for her fictitious husband. "No, I . . . merely invented him so that no one would question a young maiden traveling on her own."

"A very dangerous occupation," Lady Stenhold murmured with the first hint of reproach in her voice.

Bella shivered as she recalled the horrible moments she had spent fighting off the advances of the young officer. It had been a terrifying occurrence that still occasionally haunted her dreams. "So I discovered," she murmured.

Lady Stenhold tilted her head to one side. "Would you mind telling me why you were traveling on your own?"

"Because Lord Brasleigh is determined to marry me to Monsieur LeMont," she said bluntly.

At last Lady Stenhold appeared startled by Bella's words. Clearly she had not expected this. "Monsieur LeMont is your fiancé?"

"Not by choice." Bella's countenance hardened as she allowed her anger at Lord Brasleigh's arrogant dismissal of her future to simmer to the surface. "After my father's death, Lord Brasleigh became my guardian. Not that he was much of a guardian. Like my father, he believed that his only duty was to provide a house and pay a staff to keep me buried in the country. As long as I remained properly subdued and created no difficulties, I was happily forgotten, but the moment I refused to submit to the companionship of fools, I was swiftly thrust into an engagement with a gentleman in desperate enough straights that he would wed the devil himself if he brought a large enough dowry."

A small silence fell as Lady Stenhold pondered her low words. Bella found herself biting her lower lip. Although she felt personally insulted by Lord Brasleigh's behavior, she logically realized that he was perfectly within his rights to arrange a marriage for her. Somehow, it was important to her that Lady Stenhold not agree with the arrogant lord.

Thankfully, the older woman smiled with gentle understanding. "And so you left?"

"Yes." Bella gave a tiny grimace. "I had intended to go to London, but those soldiers frightened me, and when you suggested that I join you, it seemed the best solution to my troubles."

"I am very glad that you did," Lady Stenhold said in firm tones. "There is no telling what might have happened to you had you actually continued your journey."

A portion of Bella was not nearly so confident. Lord Brasleigh had managed to track her to Surrey, as impossible as the task might seem. Perhaps a servant had recognized her and contacted her guardian, or maybe the innkeeper had seen her enter Lady Stenhold's carriage. But it would have been a far more difficult task to have followed her had she reached London.

Still, she was not so lost to reason as to deny that the dangers she faced on the road would only have been multiplied surrounded by thousands of strangers.

The image of being alone and penniless in such a vast city sent a shiver down her spine. "I realize that now," she reluctantly admitted.

Confident that she had made her point, Lady Stenhold turned the conversation back to Bella's current difficulties. "I am curious as to why Lord Brasleigh pretended not to know who you were. Surely he came here to take you back to his home?"

Bella discovered herself shying away from revealing Lord Brasleigh's charade. Although he was the one who should feel shame at his actions, she had no desire to discuss what had occurred between them.

Especially those heart-stopping kisses . . .

"It is a long and complicated story."

Lady Stenhold's lips twitched. "Is it?"

Anxious to divert the older woman's thoughts, Bella leaned forward. "I suppose you are very angry with me?"

The older woman considered Bella's question before giving a slow shake of her head.

"No, not angry. To be honest, I had suspected that there was more to you than a mere widow. Particularly after Lord Brasleigh's arrival. I do wish, however, that you would have trusted me with the truth."

Bella gave a small blink of surprise. So, she had not been nearly as clever as she had thought. All along, Lady Stenhold had been aware that she was not being entirely truthful. A lucky thing she had not attempted to try her skills upon the stage. She would surely have starved to death.

"It was never a matter of trust," she assured her friend. "But if you had known the truth, I feared that you might feel compelled to contact my guardian."

Lady Stenhold gave a click of her tongue. "Not unless you wished me to."

"Of course, it would not have done much good either way." She gave a restless lift of her shoulder. "Lord Brasleigh somehow knew where I was the entire time."

"So, what will you do?"

"Do?"

"Will you marry Monsieur LeMont?" Lady Stenhold demanded. "He appears a kindly sort, although I regret that I cannot say the same for his mother."

Bella stiffened her spine in a determined manner. "I have no intention of marrying anyone."

"Lord Brasleigh is in the position to make such a decision."

Bella needed no such reminder. She was aggravatingly aware of Lord Brasleigh's control over her life. Unfortunately, there was precious little she could do to alter the situation. At least for the moment. "Then I will flee again, and this time I will ensure that he does not find me."

Lady Stenhold abruptly rose to her feet, her expression troubled. "Please do not act hastily, my dear. You recall what occurred at the posting inn."

Bella lifted her hands. "What else can I do?"

"Let us wait and see. Perhaps together we can convince Lord Brasleigh that you deserve better than a marriage of convenience."

Bella also rose, inwardly acknowledging that it would be easier to convince the prince regent to live upon a modest income. "He is not concerned with what is best for me," she retorted in faintly bitter tones. "He only wishes to be rid of his pledge to my father."

"Just promise me that you will do nothing without discussing it with me first," Lady Stenhold insisted.

Bella wavered, uncertain whether she was willing to give such a pledge or not. There might come a moment when she felt compelled into flight. Then, with a tiny sigh, she accepted that if she did leave, she would have to seek this woman's help. She would not flee again with no money and nowhere to go. And besides, she instinctively knew that she could trust Lady Stenhold with any trouble. "I promise."

"Thank you, my dear."

"I will leave you to finish preparing for dinner."

With an unknowingly sad smile, Bella turned and left the room. She wanted to be alone with her thoughts for the moment.

Heading downstairs, she avoided the drawing room and instead entered a small sitting room. It would soon be time for dinner, but until then she desired a bit of peace. Closing the door behind her, she stepped toward the lion-clawed sofa only to give a soft gasp as she realized that there was already a slender, dark-haired gentleman seated upon the brocade cushions.

"Oh." Her eyes widened as Monsieur LeMont politely rose to his feet. Attired in a pale blue coat and cream pantaloons, he appeared remarkably handsome. Far too handsome to need to marry for a paltry dowry, she acknowledged. Surely there must be dozens of heiresses anxious to wed such an eligible gentleman?

He performed an elegant bow. "Miss Lowe."

"I did not know anyone would be here."

"I fear you have caught me hiding out," he confessed with a rueful grin.

"Hiding?"

"I was in little mood for conversation."

She took a step backward. "Then I will leave you."

"No, please." Again he flashed that persuasive smile. "I wish you would stay."

Despite all her hard feelings toward this gentleman, Bella found that it was impossible to resist his gentle charm. There was something quite endearing about his manner. "Very well."

Crossing the carpet, she settled on the edge of the sofa. Monsieur LeMont resumed his seat beside her. "I wished for an opportunity to apologize for my mother."

"There is no need," Bella murmured.

"There is every need," he insisted. "I fear she possesses little shame in acquiring what she wants. I begged her to remain in London, but she fretted that Lord Brasleigh might change his mind while away from town."

"She need have no fear." Bella smiled wryly. "Lord Brasleigh is determined to force us into marriage."

He gave a grimace, but his tone was light. "That makes it rather awkward for us, does it not?"

"Decidedly awkward," she agreed.

For a moment he studied her tiny features. "May I be so bold as to inquire about your feelings toward a marriage between us?"

Bella was uncertain how to respond. Oddly, she discovered herself reluctant to hurt his feelings. "To be honest, I have no desire to wed anyone. I am sorry."

Surprisingly, an expression of genuine relief fluttered across his thin face.

"Do not apologize. I am no more inclined to marriage than yourself."

He did not wish to wed? Was it possible that he was no more than a pawn, just as herself? A flare of hope bloomed deep in her heart.

"Then . . . why?"

For a moment, she thought he might not answer her question; then he gave a rueful shrug. "You have met my mother. Once she discovered that Lord Brasleigh was offering a handsome dowry, there was nothing that could sway her determination that I should be chosen as the prospective bridegroom."

Bella abruptly leaned forward, her eyes unconsciously pleading. "You could always refuse."

Monsieur LeMont gave a slow shake of his head. "I have on several occasions, but my mother will not listen to reason."

Bella slowly leaned back. After meeting Madam LeMont she could well imagine her son's difficulties. Madam LeMont was every bit as tenacious and arrogant as Lord Brasleigh. Maybe even more so if that were possible. "It appears that we are in the same muddle," she retorted.

He cast her a sympathetic glance. "Yes, it does."

She lifted her hands in a helpless motion. "So, what is to be done?"

"There seems little we can do."

Her expression unconsciously became despondent. "No, I suppose not."

For a moment, he regarded her drooping lips; then he abruptly leaned forward. "Hold on. Perhaps we should consider our options."

"Options?"

A teasing glint entered his brown eyes as he pretended to ponder their dilemma. "There must be something we can do. Let us see. . . . Perhaps we could barricade ourselves in the room and refuse to come out."

A reluctant smile curved her lips as she realized that he was kindly attempting to ease her troubled spirits. Any lingering resentment toward the gentleman whom Lord Brasleigh had chosen as her bridegroom was swept aside. He was not to blame for the treachery of her guardian and his mother.

"I do not believe that one small bowl of grapes would hold us for long."

He heaved a sorrowful sigh. "I suppose you are right."

Entering into the teasing, Bella tapped a slender finger to her chin. "We could always become smugglers and live in a cave."

"I fear that caves make me sneeze," he informed her in regretful tones.

"Well, we could not have that."

He considered her another moment. "We could take to the stage. With your beauty, we would no doubt be an overwhelming success."

Bella gave a dramatic shudder. "Thank you, but I believe that I prefer the cave."

"Well, then, perhaps we will simply become highwaymen," he suggested.

Rather unbelievably, Bella discovered herself enjoying their ridiculous bantering. She had never had the companionship of those her own age. It was rather nice to have someone about who did not treat her as a child and did not twist her stomach into knots.

"Ah . . . That I like," she retorted with a saucy grin. "We could dash about the countryside and become quite legendary."

"Oh, yes. And we would chose only the most expensive coaches to plunder," he insisted.

She nodded her head in agreement. "We would be most particular."

"And our only concern would be the local magistrate."

The image of herself and this elegant young gentleman galloping across the countryside to hold up carriages with armed servants and outriders made her chuckle. "A trifling problem when compared to Lord Brasleigh and your mother."

He gave a low chuckle. "Trifling, indeed."

His laughter was still floating through the room when the door was abruptly thrust open and Lord Brasleigh stepped inside. In the blink of an eye, the frivolous atmosphere was dispelled.

Appearing annoyingly handsome in a moss-green coat and silver waistcoat, his large form easily dominated the room. He was so commanding, so utterly sure of himself. Bella gritted her teeth even as her stomach gave that odd twinge that seemed to travel to the tips of her toes.

"There you are, Bella," he said unnecessarily, his gaze taking careful note of her rather intimate position next to Monsieur LeMont.

"My lord," she retorted in clipped tones.

"Dinner is about to be served."

At his announcement, Monsieur LeMont rose to his feet. "Mother will be searching for me. Excuse me."

With a lingering smile toward Bella, the younger gentleman strolled from the room. Alone with the aggravating man, Bella rose to her feet. She felt intimidated enough without having to twist her neck to meet his narrowed silver gaze.

Lord Brasleigh watched her movements with an unreadable expression. "You appeared to be quite enjoying LeMont's company," he said abruptly.

Bella gave an indifferent shrug. "He is very charming."

Oddly, Lord Brasleigh did not appear particularly pleased with her response. "I would not have chosen him if he had not been."

She gave a disgusted snort. "You would have chosen Napoleon if it would have suited your purpose." Tilting her chin, she marched forward. "Now, excuse me. I should not wish to be late for dinner."

Twelve

The delicate strains of the pianoforte floated through the air, adding a pleasant backdrop to the muted conversation. Not that Philip found himself particularly enjoying Bella's performance. For some reason, the sight of her seated before the instrument while LeMont stood beside her to turn the pages was less than pleasing.

It was not that he did not wish the two to become better acquainted, he assured himself. After all, they would soon be wed. And he was relieved that they had not taken an instant aversion to each other. The aggravating chit was just stubborn enough to treat her fiancé with the sharp edge of her tongue.

But for all his stern reminders that matters appeared to be progressing even better than expected, he could not dismiss the flare of distaste at the air of intimacy that appeared to have bloomed in such a rapid fashion.

For goodness' sakes, LeMont was nearly draped over her side with his hand upon her shoulder, and more than once he had leaned down to whisper something in her ear.

They were not yet wed, Philip told himself with an unconscious frown. And he had not averted his ward from one scandal only to have her plunge headlong into another.

With an effort, he turned his back on the two and attempted to concentrate on Madam LeMont and Lady Stenhold seated upon a small sofa.

"It is so lovely to have music in the house again," Lady Stenhold was saying with a faint smile.

Although Philip had not yet had the opportunity to speak with Lady Stenhold and apologize for his less than gentlemanly behavior, it was obvious she had already forgiven Bella for her deceit. There was nothing but admiration in her expression as she regarded her young guest.

Madam LeMont, however, was not quite so admiring. Her long face was instead set in rather critical lines. "Yes, although I fear Miss Lowe is only an adequate musician. Luckily, I am quite talented upon the pianoforte and shall endeavor to improve her skills."

Lady Stenhold instantly bristled at the disparagement of her friend. "I think she plays quite lovely. What about you, my lord?"

"Yes," Philip retorted in ominous tones. He did not care for Madam LeMont's words any more than Lady Stenhold.

As if sensing the disapproval about her, Madam LeMont gave a forced laugh. "Oh, do not imagine that I am complaining," she protested. "Miss Lowe is quite a charming girl. But like all maidens, she will need the guidance of a more experienced lady. Without a mother, poor dear, it falls on me to lead her on the proper path."

Philip forced himself to grit his teeth at the condescending tone, but Lady Stenhold was not so discrete. "I fear that Miss Lowe does not care to be led upon any path. She can be quite headstrong."

Madam LeMont's features hardened. "That is a failing that will quickly be mended."

Lady Stenhold pursed her lips. "By you?"

"Well, Andre is of far too sweet a nature to mold a wife to his suiting," Madam LeMont retorted. "Indeed, he is often imposed upon in the most infamous manner."

"Yes, I can well believe it," Lady Stenhold said dryly.

A smug expression settled on Madam LeMont's countenance. "It shall be my duty to ensure that she is a comfortable wife."

If Philip had not been so infuriated by the vulgar woman's presumption that she was in any way qualified to school a lady of genuine breeding, he would have laughed aloud. Bella, a comfortable wife? It was absurd. She might be clever, adorable, spirited, and utterly aggravating, but she would never, ever be comfortable.

Lady Stenhold's expression echoed his own disgust as she rigidly studied the large woman. "Tell me, Madam LeMont, do you intend to reside with your son?"

Madam LeMont instantly summoned a martyred air. She even raised a lace handkerchief to dab at her nose. "Unfortunately, I was left with only a pittance of an income after the death of my beloved husband. Such a tragedy for a poor widow. I could not possibly support my own establishment and depend upon the generosity of my only son."

Philip was well aware that she was being far from truthful. He had personally investigated the LeMonts before choosing Andre, and he had discovered that Madam LeMont received a dowager's income from her husband's estate. She was more than capable of living in comfort, if not an extravagant manner. She was clearly greedy enough to wish to live on his dowry while feathering her comfort with her own income.

"How tragic," Lady Stenhold murmured, although her tone was far from sympathetic.

"And of course, Andre would be quite lost without me near," the woman continued, unaware of her audience's growing distaste. "I know precisely how to arrange his household for his comfort."

"Of course," Lady Stenhold muttered.

Philip could endure no more. Although he had realized that Madam LeMont was something of a bully, he had not allowed himself to accept just how ghastly she truly was.

How dare she presume that he would stand aside while she moved into Bella's home and played the petty tyrant? And to suggest that she could train Bella to be a lady. The sheer audacity stole his breath. Bella was a lady from the top of her golden curls to the tips of her tiny feet. While Madam LeMont was . . .

Reminding himself that he was a gentleman, Philip did not allow the thought to form. Besides, a far more disturbing thought began to wiggle in the back of his mind.

Had he not considered Madam LeMont's boorish manner because he had not been concerned with whether or not Bella was happy in her new home? Had he indeed been so anxious to rid himself of Bella that he would have offered her to Napoleon?

He drew in a sharp breath. Dash it all! It was too late for regrets. The match was made, and there was nothing he could do now.

Wishing that he could somehow retrieve the confident assurance in his infallibility that he had once accepted as his right, Philip gave a shake of his head.

Blast Bella Lowe.

"Excuse me," he muttered before turning and moving toward Lord Blackmar who had staked a place beside the tray of brandy.

Perhaps his friend could ease the peculiar sense of dissatisfaction that seemed lodged in the pit of his stomach. Coming to a halt, he accepted the brandy that his friend held out.

"You are looking particularly grim for a gentleman who has won the battle," Pudding drawled.

"Madam LeMont could make any gentleman appear grim," he muttered.

Pudding shrugged. "Once you have Miss Lowe wed, you can wash your hands of the harridan."

"I suppose."

Something in his tone made his companion regard him closely. "You are not having second thoughts, are you?"

"I merely forgot how excessively vulgar she is."

If he had not been so preoccupied, Philip might have noted the sly glint in Pudding's eyes. As it was, he was far too busy with his disturbing thoughts.

"At least the son appears to be a remarkably pleasing young man."

Philip slowly turned to regard the two in the corner. His mood was not lightened at the sight of them laughing at some private comment. "Yes, it is difficult to believe that they are related," he grudgingly conceded.

"And you must be pleased that Miss Lowe appears quite taken with him," his friend prodded.

Pleased was not at all what Philip was feeling. Still, he was in no mood to discuss his strange reaction. "They appear friendly enough."

"At least you no longer have to fear that she will bolt in the middle of the night."

Philip gave a sharp laugh. "I do not believe for a moment that Miss Lowe has so abruptly conceded defeat. She is too contrary for that, no matter how taken she might be with LeMont."

Pudding lifted his glass and pretended to study the amber liquid. "Then why do you not simply take them to Scotland and have them wed?"

Philip gazed at his friend in shock. "Do not be absurd."

"It would be a swift end to your troubles, and we would be free to return to London." Pudding turned to regard him squarely. "Miss Ravel is no doubt anxiously awaiting your return."

At the moment, Philip did not care if the actress had to wait until her hair turned gray. Or even if she waited at all. "Miss Ravel will simply have to wait," he said indifferently; then as a movement flickered in the corner of his eye, he abruptly turned his head to discover LeMont calmly escorting Bella through the open French doors and into the garden. "What the devil?"

Without even glancing toward Pudding, Philip was stalking across the room and through the doors. How dare they simply quit the room in such a fashion? Did they believe their disappearance would go unnoticed? Or was Bella once again attempting to goad him into Bedlam?

He discovered the pair just about to step onto a narrow path that would lead them to a rarely used section of the garden. Philip felt a flare of annoyance at their lack of propriety.

"Monsieur LeMont," he said loudly, watching as they halted and reluctantly turned to face him.

"Yes, my lord?"

"I must beg that you return to the others. I have need to speak with my ward alone."

"Of course." Seemingly indifferent to Philip's narrowed gaze, Andre lifted Bella's slender hand to kiss her fingers. "We will speak later."

A silence fell as the young man slowly strolled back to the house. Then, once they were alone, Bella turned to regard him with her familiar dislike. "What do you want?"

Want? He gazed down at her mutinous expression. He wanted to pull her into his arms and kiss her until her anger melted and she pressed that delectable form next to his own.

As soon as the treacherous thought entered his head he was scrubbing it away. He was clearly losing what few senses he still had left. "Although it should not be necessary, I thought it only prudent to remind you that it is hardly proper for you to be wandering through a dark garden with a young gentleman."

He heard her sharp intake of breath. "Improper to spend a few moments with my fiancé? I thought you wished me to be with Monsieur LeMont in a far more intimate setting than a dark garden."

His gut twisted at her direct thrust. No, he would not consider such things. He could not. "You are determined to create a scandal," he gritted.

"I am alone with you now. Are you not terrified of a scandal?" she taunted.

"I am your guardian."

"You have yet to act like my guardian."

He was uncomfortably aware of that fact. No matter how good his intentions, he always seemed to end up behaving badly. He regarded her with frustration. "What would you have me do?"

"I only wished to be treated as a young lady with

a bit of intelligence, not as a piece of property to be disposed of."

"I have never considered you a piece of property."

"No?"

Philip refused to consider whether the scent of lavender came from the garden or Bella's golden curls as he stepped closer.

"Most guardians wish to see their wards suitably married."

"To complete strangers?" she demanded.

"Would you prefer a season in town to meet eligible gentlemen?" The words were out before he could halt them. For goodness' sakes, the last thing he wanted was to play escort from one dreary affair to another. Still, he made no attempt to detract them.

She appeared unimpressed by his impulsive words. "Once I would have been happy to come to London for such a season. All I have ever desired was to fall in love and have a family."

"Love?" he said in startled tones.

"Yes? Is that so surprising? I have had precious little of it in my life."

"Nonsense. Your father loved you."

She gave a restless wave of her hand. "Did he?"

"Yes. He often spoke of you when we were together."

"My father did not even know me. On the few occasions he was home, he barely recalled that I was about."

It was all too easy to imagine the lonely little girl forlornly awaiting a bit of attention. Colonel Lowe, after all, had been away from home a great deal, and he certainly was not an overly emotional sort of gentleman. He would not have found it easy to re-

veal his love to his daughter. Philip's expression unknowingly softened. "Perhaps he merely found it
difficult to express his feelings."

She gave a sudden shrug. "It hardly matters
now."

Instinctively, his hand raised to brush her soft
cheek. "Bella . . ."

With a jerky movement she stepped away. "I am
tired, sir. Please excuse me."

She slipped away before he could halt her, and
with a heavy sigh, Philip turned toward the dark
garden.

Colonel Lowe had a great deal to answer for.

Awakening early the next morning, Bella deliberately chose the servant's stairs to make her way out
of the house. It was not that she feared encounter-
ing Lord Brasleigh, she assured herself. She simply
wished to enjoy a walk without the company of her
guardian or even Andre. And of course, no one
could fault her for wishing to avoid the poisonous
company of Madam LeMont.

Entering the kitchen garden, Bella made a direct
path toward the distant woods. Thankfully, it was
another lovely day, and she soon found her spirits
lifting as she strolled through the outdoors, sunshine warming her skin.

How could anyone fail to appreciate the deep
blue of the sky and the warmth of the morning
sun—even if she had lain awake most of the long
night? Determined to enjoy her brief privacy, Bella
absently began to gather the wildflowers along the
path. Suddenly, a faint sound behind a nearby bush
caught her attention.

Attempting to convince herself that it was nothing more sinister than a small animal, she pushed her way forward only to halt in horror.

Lord Brasleigh. Heaven above, was he everywhere?

Quite prepared to turn and flee, she was halted as he lifted his head and stabbed her with a glittering gaze. "Come here," he commanded.

At first she had presumed that he had been sitting upon the mossy ground to enjoy the tranquil morning, but Bella slowly realized that he was leaning over something on the ground. A flare of curiosity made her ignore the tiny voice that warned her to dismiss his imperative order. "What is it?" she demanded.

"Someone has laid a trap," he informed her in clipped tones.

With a puzzled frown, she slowly rounded his form to discover a large hound stretched upon the ground with his back leg caught in a savage trap.

"Oh." She gave a small cry and sank to her knees. "The poor dog."

"I want you to try to keep him calm while I free him."

Bella for once offered no arguments. Instead, she reached out her hands to gently stroke the dog's head. Her heart twisted with pain as the animal attempted to give a wag of his tail.

"Such a good boy," she murmured, her fear deepening as the dog barely moved despite Lord Brasleigh's efforts to pry open the trap. "He is so weak."

"A curse upon poachers," Lord Brasleigh muttered as he struggled with the trap. "Just one more moment."

"Please hurry."

"I do not wish to injure him further," he warned.

She held her breath as Lord Brasleigh battled the evil trap. For the moment, she forgot that she intensely disliked the man at her side. Nothing mattered but that they save the poor creature. "Who would do such a thing?" she demanded.

"I shall certainly be sure the magistrate discovers that with all possible speed." He gave a sudden murmur of satisfaction as the trap sprang free. "There."

Bella studied the battered leg that was seeping blood in an alarming quantity.

"Will he live?" she whispered.

"I do not know." Shrugging out of his coat, he handed it toward her; then with a rueful smile, he determinedly began unfastening his linen shirt. "Forgive me, but I must stop the bleeding."

"Of course."

Bella attempted to concentrate on the dog that lay dangerously still on the ground, as Philip tugged off his shirt and gently tied it about the wounded leg. Not that she was wholly successful. How did any maiden ignore a large male form stripped to the waist? Particularly when those firm muscles rippled in such a disturbing fashion beneath the silken skin.

Still, her concern for the dog allowed her to rise to her feet as Lord Brasleigh gathered the animal in his arms and straightened.

"We must get him to the stables," he commanded, already thrusting his way through the bushes and onto the path.

Bella was swift to follow in his wake. Together they silently moved toward the main building, skirting the house and heading directly for the stables. They had barely stepped into the shadowed interior when the head groom met them.

"My lord." The rather battered old servant with gray hair and a heavily lined face regarded them with a frown.

"He was caught in a trap," Lord Brasleigh said in clipped tones as he brushed past the groom to place the dog upon a pile of straw in an empty stall.

Bella and the servant followed the distracted lord.

"A trap?" the groom growled, his frown only deepening. He lifted a hand toward a hovering groom who instantly hurried forward. "Duncan, go fetch the magistrate and then organize a search of the grounds. I won't have a bloody poacher on my land."

"At once." The under groom gave a nod of his head before turning and hurrying out of the stables.

Clearly satisfied that his commands would be obeyed, the groom kneeled beside the dog and carefully removed Lord Brasleigh's hasty binding.

"A nasty wound," he muttered.

"He has lost a lot of blood," Lord Brasleigh agreed.

Once again rising to his feet, the groom scratched his head. "We'll wrap the wound with a poultice. There is little more we can do."

He left the stall to retrieve the wrapping, and Bella moved to kneel beside Lord Brasleigh. Her arm brushed the silken heat of his bare skin, but she grimly ignored the tiny shivers it sent through her blood.

Turning his head, he regarded her with a faint sense of surprise, as if he presumed she had scurried from him the moment she was able. "You should return to the house," he murmured.

Her expression became stubborn. "I want to stay."

He arched a raven brow. "I did not think you wished to spend a moment more in my company than absolutely necessary."

"I am not remaining for you. My only concern is for this dog."

He gave a low chuckle. "I am flattered."

Before she could retort, the groom was returning and efficiently kneeling down to grasp the wounded leg. The dog stirred enough to try to kick from his grasp.

"Hold him steady, my lord."

Lord Brasleigh pushed gently on the dog's side. "Bella, talk to him."

Leaning down, Bella began to coo soft words into the dog's ear, feeling a pang of sympathy at the faint whines that drifted through the straw-scented air.

At last the groom sat back on his heels. "It's done."

Lord Brasleigh gave a nod of his head. "If we can avoid an infection, I believe it will heal."

"Aye, although I be more worried about his loss of blood."

"Yes."

"I'll go to the kitchen and get some scraps from Cook to tempt him," the groom offered, rising to his feet and once again disappearing from the stall.

With the immediate danger over, Bella was suddenly conscious she was quite alone with Lord Brasleigh. And more disturbing—he was nearly half naked. A most potent combination.

She straightened, feeling strangely awkward.

"You did well," Lord Brasleigh commended, his gaze stroking over her pale features.

"So did you," she grudgingly conceded. Whatever her feelings for this gentleman, she could not deny that he had reacted with more gentle concern for the dog than any other gentleman she knew. "If he lives, it will be because of you."

His hand slowly rose to stroke the full curve of her lower lip. "Perhaps I am not the unfeeling beast you have labeled me."

A scalding heat raced through her body and with awkward haste Bella surged to her feet.

Why, oh, why did she long to trace the firm line of his broad chest? To press her lips to the heat of his mouth? It made no sense. No sense at all.

"I am not so easily convinced, my lord," she assured him in breathless tones.

Then, turning on her heel, she forced herself to march away without a backward glance.

Thirteen

Feeling far too restless to return to the house, Bella instead angled toward the newly scythed grounds. Her feet instinctively carried her toward the pretty grotto, even as her thoughts remained firmly centered on the gentleman she had left in the stables. What an aggravating mystery he was. One moment arrogant, the next a playful tease, and then without warning, unnervingly tender.

He had not pretended his concern for the injured dog. He had clearly been distraught at the grievous injury the animal had received and equally furious at the poacher who had left the trap. Such gentle concern was echoed in his treatment of poor Miss Summers. As well as in his patience with his supposedly overbearing mother.

So why then did he treat her with such a boorish indifference to her feelings?

She clenched her teeth in frustration.

It should not concern her how he treated her. He was nothing more than an unwelcome intruder in her life, and soon she would discover a means of ridding herself of his annoying presence once and for all.

The thought should have brought a smile to her face. Instead her heart felt heavier than ever.

Exasperated at her unpredictable emotions, she climbed the steps to the grotto, only to discover Andre already seated on a marble bench inside. "Andre. May I join you?"

He politely rose to his feet with a smile. "Of course."

Waiting for Bella to take her seat, Andre lowered himself beside her.

"It is a lovely view, is it not?" she inquired as she gazed at the terraced garden and sparkling fountains spread before them.

"Yes, it is," Andre agreed.

"Lady Stenhold claims that she encountered Lord Stenhold for the first time at this precise location. She had come to visit his sister, and when they met, they fell instantly in love. He later had this grotto built to honor that moment."

"Very romantic," Andre murmured.

It was romantic, Bella acknowledged. How would it feel to glance into a gentleman's eyes and know in a heartbeat that he was the man she wished to wed?

For no reason at all, the dark countenance of Lord Brasleigh seared through her thoughts. She hurriedly thrust it aside.

"Do you believe in love at first sight?" She turned to glance at Andre, speaking more out of a desire to keep her renegade thoughts at bay than to pry into her companion's private affairs.

Surprisingly, his thin features hardened at her question. "Yes."

"You sound very certain."

"Because it happened to me."

"Really?" she breathed, instantly intrigued. "Who is she?"

Andre grimaced, his eyes darkening with remembered loss. "You cannot wish to hear the tragic tale of my lost love."

Shoving aside her inner troubles, Bella reached out to grasp his hand with an expression of concern. "I do want to hear it, very much," she assured him. "What is her name?"

He paused before a reminiscent smile curved his lips. "Claudette Movane. We met in London after Mother and I left France. Like us, she comes from a family that was forced to flee the ravages of war. And like us, she was left with little more than the memories of her family's past glory."

Bella felt a tiny pang of sympathy. How difficult it must be to leave behind family and friends. It was little wonder Andre would find himself drawn to a young maiden who reminded him of his past. "Is she very beautiful?"

"Not as beautiful as you." His expression became whimsical. "But she is sweet and kind and always wishing to make others happy."

"She sounds delightful," Bella said sincerely, unfortunately aware that no one could describe her in such an admirable manner. She seemed perfect for the sensitive Andre. "Why did you not wed?"

His smile slowly fled. "Because our families forbade the match."

"But why?"

"We are expected to replenish our families' coffers."

Bella had no difficulty in imagining Madam LeMont's shrill demands that her son provide her with suitable comfort. She would never consider for a moment Andre's own happiness. It would be his duty to make whatever sacrifices necessary.

"I see," she said quietly.

Clearly misunderstanding her faint frown, Andre was swift to dismiss any hint of insult. "Forgive me, Bella. It is not that I do not find you a most beautiful and charming maiden. Indeed, I find that I like you far more than I could ever have expected. And if not for Claudette, I might even have come to love you."

Bella gave a soft laugh. "Please do not apologize, Andre. I believe that we have become friends enough for the truth between us."

He heaved a grateful sigh. "I like to hope we are friends."

She turned her thoughts back to his obvious troubles. "Is there no hope for you?"

"No." He gave a sad shake of his head. "Mother is determined to see that I acquire a dowry and, of course, Claudette's family is anxiously searching for a title and fortune to restore their place in society."

"It is all so unfair," Bella blurted out, unable to bear the thought of Andre being shoved into a loveless marriage, even with herself. How could those who were suppose to care for them be so heartless?

"What of you?"

Momentarily lost in thought, Bella was unprepared for the abrupt question. "What?"

"Is there someone you love?"

For no reason at all, Bella felt a blush crawl beneath her cheeks. "No. I have met very few gentlemen."

Andre regarded her for a long moment. "What of Lord Brasleigh?"

"Lord Brasleigh?" She instinctively stiffened. "Whatever do you mean?"

Andre shrugged. "He is very possessive of you."

"He is my guardian," she pointed out with unnecessary force.

"When he is gazing at you, I do not believe he is recalling that he is your guardian."

Bella abruptly pulled her hand from his fingers. Heavens above, was Andre implying that Lord Brasleigh possessed an . . . interest in her? Surely Andre had bumped his head or eaten a bad piece of meat. That could be the only excuse for such a ludicrous accusation. "That is absurd."

Undaunted, Andre shifted so that he could more easily study her heated countenance. "Is it? Tell me, Bella, has he ever kissed you?"

Bella swallowed an hysterical urge to laugh. The chaste meeting of lips that she had once considered to be kisses had nothing at all in common with the fiercely exciting embraces that Lord Brasleigh had bestowed upon her. Not that she was about to make such a confession to anyone. Nor the fact that those embraces were never far from her thoughts.

"Yes, but not because he wanted to," she reluctantly muttered.

Andre's laughter floated through the grotto. "Oh, Bella, for all your spirit, you are remarkably innocent. No man kisses a maiden unless he wishes to."

Bella stubbornly gazed at the fingers clenched in her lap. She did not want to ponder why she was avoiding his probing glance.

"I do not understand what you are attempting to imply."

"I cannot help but wonder if a portion of the turmoil between you and Lord Brasleigh is not from an unwanted attraction."

A tiny shiver inched down her spine. "You could not be further from the truth."

"No?"

"No," she insisted, refusing to consider the notion. She had already accepted that she was far too aware of Lord Brasleigh than was reasonable; she would not push herself any further. "Lord Brasleigh has never considered me as anything more than an unwelcome burden. Why else would he have offered you such a large dowry to be rid of me?"

Andre was indifferent to her logic. "Perhaps he is beginning to regret his offer."

Bella awkwardly surged to her feet. She might genuinely like Andre, but she could not discuss the peculiar tension between herself and Lord Brasleigh. "You clearly are determined to be a tease."

With a rueful smile, Andre rose to his feet. "I am sorry, Bella."

She shrugged, anxious to divert his thoughts to less troublesome matters. "Shall we take a stroll about the lake?"

The silence of the stables was a welcome relief after an hour of enduring Madam LeMont's shrill conversation. Really, the woman was enough to make a saint long to throttle her, Bella thought as she crossed to enter the stall and kneel beside the waiting dog. Throughout the tedious lunch, the large woman had tortured them with a droning lecture on the evils of the Almack's patronesses who had refused to offer her vouchers, and the dastardly landlord who possessed the audacity to demand rent from his social betters. It had been all Bella could do to resist pointing out that the landlord no doubt had a family to feed, and unlike her, did not depend upon others to pamper to his selfish needs.

Instead, she had turned her thoughts to Andre's outrageous suggestions that there was more between herself and Lord Brasleigh than angry discord. Why could she not laugh it aside? It was ridiculous, of course. Beyond ridiculous.

And yet, her every attempt to thrust aside the absurd thought was thwarted as it niggled its way firmly back to the surface, regardless of her efforts.

It had been a decided relief when the meal came to an end and she was free to quietly slip from the room. Lady Stenhold was far too perceptive not to eventually notice her uncommon silence. She did not want the older woman probing for explanations.

Bella absently stroked the soft fur of the dog, smiling as his tail thumped upon the straw in happiness. At least this poor beast appeared to be on the mend. Nothing short of a miracle, considering he had been but a breath from dying.

It was the shadow falling across the straw that alerted her that her peace was about to come to an abrupt end. Her heart faltered at the growingly familiar tingle that raced through her body. She had no need to turn her head to know that Lord Brasleigh was standing just behind her.

"I thought I might find you here," he said, moving to place himself on the straw beside her.

Bella struggled to conjure the prickly distaste that she used to keep this gentleman at a firm distance, but for once it remained decidedly elusive. Instead, she nervously plucked at the folds of her skirt as if she were an uncertain schoolgirl. And it was all because of Andre's foolish questions, she inwardly stewed.

With an effort to distract that lingering silver gaze, she spoke the first words that came to her mind. "Your patient appears much improved."

A satisfied smile curved his firm lips. "Oh, yes, Nelson is quite a brave soldier."

"Nelson?" she questioned in puzzlement.

"Well, his previous name was Pug, hardly a heroic title."

"No, indeed."

"Here." With a swift movement, he untied the small bundle he held in his hands. Nelson gave a yelp of sheer pleasure as Lord Brasleigh offered him a delicate meat pastry. "He has developed a decided preference for pheasant pie."

Although Bella had only encountered Lady Stenhold's cook on a handful of occasions, the imposing lady had not struck her as a woman with a particular soft spot for animals. "Cook actually made pheasant pie for a dog?"

A rather wicked glint entered his eyes. "I did not exactly inquire if it was for Nelson."

"You stole it," she accused.

"Nothing of the sort. I simply found it on the counter and presumed that Cook would be delighted to aid in this fine boy's recovery."

Bella could not suppress a renegade smile that twitched at her lips. "She would have your head on a platter if she realized you were filching her creations for a mere dog."

"Ah, but this is no mere dog." Lord Brasleigh reached out to gently pat Nelson's head, sending its tail wagging in sheer ecstasy. Clearly the wise dog was well aware of who he owed his life to. "He is a survivor."

Bella felt a peculiar warmth spread through her heart, and barely aware of her movement, she reached out to stroke her hands over the soft fur of the dog. She was vibrantly aware of his slender fingers close to her own. "Yes, he is."

"I think that he remembers your touch," he said softly, his gaze stroking over her countenance. "But then, who could forget it?"

She felt lost in the shimmering silver of his eyes. Her breath locked in her throat as a flood of pleasure raced through her body. What was happening to her? she wondered in panic. She was furious with this man. He had interfered, bullied, and lied to her from the beginning. But over the past few days it was not anger she felt when he was near, but . . . desire.

"My lord . . ." she breathed.

As if conscious of her turmoil, Lord Brasleigh slowly leaned toward her. "Yes, my dear?"

Lost in each other, neither noticed the arrival of the young footman until he discretely cleared his throat. "Excuse me, my lord."

As if caught in a compromising situation, both Bella and Lord Brasleigh scrambled to their feet. It was Lord Brasleigh, however, who regained command of his composure first and stepped out of the stall.

"What is it?"

"A message has come for you." The footman handed the folded paper to the towering lord and with a hasty bow disappeared as swiftly as he had arrived.

Struggling to regain command of herself, Bella watched as Lord Brasleigh scanned the brief missive and then crumpled it into a small ball. "Blast."

With a frown, Bella instinctively stepped closer. "Is something the matter?"

"It is from my mother."

"She is not ill, is she?"

A wry smile twisted his lips. "My mother takes great pains to ensure that she is always ill."

Bella was taken aback by his odd words. "I beg your pardon?"

"A poor attempt at a jest," he apologized; then he drew in a deep breath. "My mother is simply a lonely woman who depends upon me to care for her."

Lord Blackmar's earlier condemnation of Lady Brasleigh rose to Bella's mind. He had claimed that the older woman demanded constant attention from her only child, and that Lord Brasleigh endured it with few complaints. Once again she felt that odd twitch in the region of her heart. "And you do not mind?" she asked softly.

He shrugged, his features for once lacking that arrogance that set her teeth on edge. "My mother is alone in the world. She was never close to her family, and she never cared for moving in fashionable circles. Her entire life was centered upon my father, and when he died, she turned to me."

Bella slowly moved closer. "It is a great responsibility."

"Yes," he agreed, gazing down at her with an odd expression. "At times I regret that I do not have a dozen siblings to help keep her occupied, but there is only me."

There was something very intimate in the manner he was regarding her, as if there were no one in the world but the two of them. Bella shivered, knowing she must do something to lighten the mood or find herself clutched in his arms. God only knew what might occur if she allowed that to happen. "Perhaps you should hire her a companion," she forced herself to quip.

Thankfully her teasing brought a rueful smile to those dark features. "Brat," he retorted. "I still do not believe they were all as disreputable as you claim."

Bella grimaced. "I assure you they were worse than I could possibly describe."

"Why did you not write to tell me your troubles?" he demanded.

She shrugged, recalling the number of times she had set down to write to her indifferent guardian only to realize that it was a futile cause. "What would you have done?"

"I would have ensured that my secretary take more care in choosing your companions."

"No." She gave a sad shake of her head. "You would have branded me a meddlesome chit and promptly sought a means of unloading me from your conscience."

Her thrust slid home, and Lord Brasleigh gave a visible flinch. Perhaps he was not completely indifferent to his arrogant dismissal of her, she told herself.

He lifted his hands in a helpless motion. "I will admit that I have never quite known what to do with a ward."

Bella readily agreed. He had certainly blundered in his choice of companions and then in his insistence that she wed Andre. But then, she couldn't deny that she had never attempted to make his role any easier. She had not wanted companions, or even to leave her father's tiny estate.

"You could have left me in peace," she suggested softly.

His brows instantly snapped together. "Allow a young maiden to live on her own on a crumbling estate?"

She shrugged. "I was happy there. Much happier than when my father would ship me from one household to another, and certainly happier than when you insisted that I travel to your home."

"You were alone."

Her lips twisted. "I am accustomed to being alone."

Without warning, his eyes darkened, and he reached out to gently cup her cheek. "You should not be alone, Bella," he said in husky tones. "You are a woman who should have a husband to love and a dozen children."

A sharp, painfully vivid image of herself as this man's wife, holding his children, seared through her mind. He would be a passionate, fiercely loyal husband, and a father who would shower his children with love. Most importantly she would never be alone again. . . .

Then, just as shockingly swift as the image rose to mind, she was jerking away from his poignant touch. Lord Brasleigh was not suggesting that she become his wife. For goodness' sakes, he considered her no more than a pest. Instead, he was speaking of Andre, who would take her out of his life and allow him to return to London without another thought.

A wrenching pain flared through her heart as Bella at last accepted the ghastly truth. Somehow, some way, her willful heart had tumbled into love with the one gentleman she could never have.

"You mean Andre," she stated bitterly, her eyes black with her inner distress. "You are nothing if not predictable, my lord."

As if caught off guard by her fierce reaction, Lord Brasleigh frowned in concern and stepped toward her. "Bella . . ."

"No." She gave a shake of her head as she abruptly bolted for the door. "Just leave me alone."

Fourteen

It wasn't possible.

It couldn't be possible.

Women did not fall in love with gentlemen who treated them as children and handed them over to perfect strangers. And they certainly didn't love gentlemen who would subject them to such a deceitful charade.

Of course, a renegade voice whispered in the back of her mind, they did love gentlemen who accepted their responsibilities and attempted to fulfill their promises. And they loved gentlemen who made them tremble with delight at their slightest touch.

Bella sucked in a steadying breath as she rushed toward the house. It did not matter how ridiculous her emotions might be, the important thing now was to decide what she would do.

One thing was for certain. She could no longer remain at Mayfield if Lord Brasleigh were to stay. How could she, when her every glance, her every word might give away her awful secret? It would be unbearable if Lord Brasleigh were to discover the truth. Utterly unbearable.

But what was she to do?

Hoping to avoid the other guests, Bella bypassed the front courtyard and instead headed for a side garden. As a rule, most of the household retired in the late afternoon, to rest before dinner. Especially on this afternoon when they would be expected to appear at their best for the upcoming ball. Still, she did not wish to take any risk.

Predictably, her efforts were in vain. She had barely passed the arbor when Lady Stenhold wandered along the pathway from the terrace. It took only one glance at Bella's flushed countenance to realize that there was something wrong.

"Oh, dear," the older woman murmured with a hint of sympathy.

Bella felt her heart sink as she realized that there was no avoiding the encounter. "Lady Stenhold."

"I sense that you have had yet another spirited encounter with Lord Brasleigh."

There was no point in denying the truth. Who else could bring a flush to her cheeks and the combative light of battle to her eyes? She could only hope that the older woman presumed her distress was due to anger.

"The man is impossible," she muttered.

"He is still insisting that you wed Monsieur LeMont?"

An unconscious hand rose to press to her wounded heart. Who would have thought that unrequited love could cause such pain? All the great poets made it sound like a sweet, melancholy affair, not this throbbing ache in the center of her being.

"Of course."

"And how do you feel about him?"

Just for a moment, Bella's heart gave a sudden jolt; then she realized that the older woman had not been referring to Lord Brasleigh. "Oh . . . You mean Andre?"

"Yes."

Bella shrugged. "I like him very much."

"But you do not love him?"

"No."

Lady Stenhold gazed at her with a shrewd smile. "Because you love Lord Brasleigh."

A shocked silence descended as Bella gazed at the older woman in disbelief. Heavens above, was the woman one of those mystics able to divine a person's very thoughts?

Had she not been so stunned, she would have fiercely denied the accusation. After all, the fewer people who realized her feelings, the better. But her scrambled thoughts did not allow for such deception. "How did you know?"

Lady Stenhold smiled in a kindly fashion. "You do not reach my advanced years without learning a thing or two about love."

Bella wrapped her arms about her waist, feeling utterly vulnerable. It was not a pleasant feeling for a brash, always fearless young lady.

"It is all so horrible," she admitted.

"No, my dear." Lady Stenhold reached out a hand to firmly grasp her arm. "Love is never horrible. Perhaps inconvenient at times."

Inconvenient? Bella swallowed a panicked urge to laugh. Tearing a hem was inconvenient. Losing a favorite locket or being caught in the rain was inconvenient. Falling in love with Lord Brasleigh was near insanity.

"I do not know how it occurred." She gave a restless shake of her head. "One moment I was hating him for his interference in my life, and the next

I realized that I wished him to pull me into his arms and never let me go."

Lady Stenhold did not appear remotely shocked by her confession. Instead, she smiled with a rather strange satisfaction. "The greatest loves often begin that way."

This time Bella could not halt her laugh at the ridiculous words. "This is no great love, just a hopeless one."

"Oh, I would not say that."

"I would," Bella retorted firmly, not giving herself the slightest opportunity to believe in fanciful notions. She might be unable to control her unruly heart, but she was still in control of her dubious mind. "Lord Brasleigh considers me as nothing more than his ward. Besides, he is determined to see me wed in a matter of weeks."

An expression that might have been disappointment settled upon the older woman's countenance. "Well, we cannot have that," she stated in firm tones.

Bella glanced at her in surprise. "What do you mean?"

"Do you recall that I mentioned my younger sister?"

Bella gave a slow nod of her head. In truth, she was in little mood to hear reminisces of Lady Stenhold's past, but she was far too fond of her companion to try to halt her. After all, she was the only one in the entire world who actually cared for her.

"Yes, of course."

Lady Stenhold allowed a fond smile to curve her lips. "Like you, she was very beautiful, and unfortunately, my parents contracted a suitable husband for her before she had ever left the schoolroom. I was already wed and away from home or I most

certainly would have protested. Sadly, Rose was of
far too sweet a nature to go against my parents
wishes, and she wed a most ill-natured and harsh
gentleman. She never protested, but I watched her
fade away year after year." There was a faint pause
as Lady Stenhold struggled with her emotions. "She
died when she was barely forty."

Bella reached out instinctively to pat her shoulder. She was beginning to realize why Lady Stenhold had been so swift to lend her a helping hand.
She obviously regretted not saving her sister, so she
would save Bella instead. "I am so sorry."

"Yes." The older woman abruptly squared her
shoulders. "I did nothing for Rose, but I will not
allow you to suffer the same fate." Her expression
softened. "Not that I would ever compare Monsieur
LeMont with my sister's husband."

The faintest flare of hope stirred to life deep in
Bella's heart. She would trust this woman with her
life. "What can be done?"

"I have a friend who lives in London. I am certain she would agree to keep you hidden at her
house until you reach your majority."

Bella caught her breath. She would be away from
Lord Brasleigh. Granted, he would be near, but he
could hardly conduct a search of every home in
London, and if she were careful not to be seen at
any of the more fashionable places, she should be
safe. At least until she came of age and Lord
Brasleigh was no longer in the position to interfere.

Then her rising excitement was suddenly damp-
ened as logic seeped through her thoughts. "London." She gave a shake of her head. "I cannot get
to London without Lord Brasleigh following me. I
am certain that he is having me watched."

Lady Stenhold frowned. "Yes, that could be a challenge."

Bella was not about to give up without a fight. There had to be some means of getting to London. She could not be so close to safety and be halted by such a small problem.

With an effort, she turned her energies to solving the dilemma. She could not simply flee. Over the past few days, she had become increasingly aware of the same men scattered about the estate with seeming nonchalance. Even the most avid fisherman did not remain at the same spot day after day. Which meant that she would certainly be caught before she had reached the nearest village. And she could not demand to go to London without arousing unwanted suspicion.

Unless . . .

A slow, utterly wonderful thought began to bloom in her mind. What if she gave Lord Brasleigh precisely what he desired?

If she agreed to a marriage with Andre, there would be no reason to remain at Mayfield. They would go to London, and once there, it would be a simple matter to sneak off to Lady Stenhold's friend. It would also be a perfect opportunity to help Andre.

If only she could get him to agree.

"I have it," she muttered out loud.

"What is it, my dear?"

"I will explain later. First I must find Andre."

With a hasty smile for her friend, Bella continued up the path and into the house. She could only hope that Andre had not yet retired to his rooms. She wished to have his agreement without delay. The sooner she was away from Lord Brasleigh, the better.

It took several long moments before she at last discovered the young gentleman in the conservatory. He politely rose as Bella entered and hurried across the flagstone floor to join him.

"Bella."

Not bothering with polite chatter, she grasped his arm. "I believe I have the means of saving both of us."

Not surprisingly, he gazed at her as if she might be a bit off in the head. "What do you mean?"

Bella forced herself to take a moment and gather her composure. Andre would never agree if she were babbling like an idiot. "Tell me, Andre, would you marry Claudette if you could?"

"Of course," he reluctantly conceded. "But we both know that is impossible."

"Nothing is impossible," she insisted. "Have you ever considered eloping?"

His eyes widened at her shocking question. Bella was well aware that she was once again behaving in a decidedly unlady-like fashion, but she was too desperate to care. A modest maiden would have already discovered herself bullied into marriage—a fate Bella intended to avoid at all cost.

Andre at last gave a tiny shrug. "Claudette wished to do so, but I could not expose her to such scandal."

Bella waved aside his lofty morals. Principals were all very well, but there were times when the cost was too high. "What is a brief bit of gossip when compared to a life of misery?" she demanded.

He gave a slow shake of his head, clearly reluctant to dredge up his buried pain. "Even if we did, I have no fortune to support us."

Bella swallowed a sigh of exasperation. For one illogical moment, the image of Lord Brasleigh rose to her mind. He would never allow conventions and expectations to keep him from the woman he loved. He would charge into her life and sweep her into his arms without regard to what others might think. She swiftly banished the unnerving thought. Andre was of a far too malleable nature to make such a stand. At least, not without a bit of prodding.

"Perhaps you should consider supporting yourself," she carefully suggested.

His brows drew together as he allowed himself to consider her words. "You mean to have a career?"

"Is that so much worse than losing the woman you love?"

There was a long silence, and for a moment Bella feared the timid young man would decide that her suggestion was too daring. After all, it would not be easy for them to turn their backs on their families and social positions. It would be a high price to pay, even for love.

But just as she prepared herself for disappointment, a slow smile curved his lips. "There is my cousin. He offered me a position at his bank, but of course, Mother forbid me from even considering his request."

"It is a beginning," she softly encouraged him.

He abruptly grimaced. "Mother."

Bella shuddered to think how the overbearing woman would react to learning that her son had eloped with a penniless miss and intended to work in a bank. Still, the woman could not be any more unendurable than she was now. Andre might as well have one woman in his life that loved and cared for him.

"Yes, she would be gravely disappointed, but you cannot live your whole life to please her."

"She does have her own income," he murmured.

Bella smiled wryly. "I would also suggest that you choose a home without an extra bedchamber."

"What?" It took him a moment to realize her meaning. "Oh . . . yes."

Feeling a prick of guilt at her unkind regard for Madam LeMont, Bella turned her thoughts to more important matters. "So you will consider my idea?"

"Of course. It is what I want more than anything," he said in low tones. "But what of you?"

A mysterious smile curved her lips. "I do have plans, but first I must get to London."

"As do I," he agreed, not pressing her for further details of her own future. "But I do not see how that will be possible. Lord Brasleigh is likely to have us both thrown into the nearest dungeon when we confess there is to be no marriage."

Bella's smile widened. "But we are not going to confess."

"No?"

"No. We are going to announce that we wish to go to London to prepare for our wedding."

Much to his valet's dismay, Lord Brasleigh had thrust aside the valet's efforts to produce a gloriously complicated knot in his cravat and instead settled for a simple style that was reflected in the unadorned black coat and formal knee breeches he had chosen for the evening's entertainment.

He had not been looking forward to the dinner and modest ball that Lady Stenhold had insisted upon hosting. He had been a guest at such rural homes in the past and discovered that the local neighbors often treated him with an uncomfortable awe or encroaching friendliness that set his teeth on edge. But throughout the day, he could not deny a growing anticipation.

More than once he had attempted to convince himself that it was nothing more than a natural desire for a bit of entertainment. What gentleman wouldn't be eager for conversation and dancing after so many days in the country? Especially a gentleman accustomed to the endless delights of London.

But as many times as he attempted to reassure himself that it was all quite reasonable, he couldn't entirely deny that in the back of his mind was the delicious image of waltzing across the floor with Bella in his arms. With a sharp shake of his head, Philip left his chambers and made his way down the long flight of stairs. He was obviously in need of returning to London where beautiful women were ripe for the plucking.

On the point of heading to the front drawing room, he halted when the door to the library was opened and Bella stepped into the hall. Although he had seen her only a few hours before, he discovered his breath catching in his throat at the sight of her attired in a shimmering champagne gown that floated like a mist of gold about her tiny frame.

She was so lovely.

Achingly, heart-stoppingly lovely.

With an effort, he attempted to concentrate on her words. For goodness' sakes, he was not some moonling in his first throes of calf love.

"My lord, may I have a moment alone with you?"

He raised his brows in surprise. "Egad. You wish to speak with me alone? I almost fear what you might have to say."

Surprisingly, she failed to rise to his bait and instead regarded him with a steady gaze.

"Actually, I believe you will be quite pleased with my announcement."

A twinge of genuine unease stirred in his heart. She wished to please him? The world must be coming to an end. "Very well. Shall we step back into the library?"

"Yes."

Turning, she entered the vast room and moved to perch stiffly on the edge of a sofa. Philip's unease only deepened.

"A brandy?" he inquired.

"No, thank you."

"I think I should have something to fortify me." Philip headed directly for the sideboard to pour himself a healthy measure before turning to face Bella. "So, what is this announcement?"

He heard her draw in a deep breath. "I wish to tell you that I have had a change of heart."

"A change of heart?"

"Yes."

"In regard to what?"

"To my marriage to Andre."

Philip nearly dropped his glass at her shocking words. "You must be jesting."

Her gaze never wavered. "Not at all."

Philip carefully set aside the brandy, his stomach clenching with an odd sense of dread. For weeks he had battled this willful minx, determined to see her wed. The mission had indeed taken over his entire life. Now, he regarded her with a wary disbelief. "This is very sudden."

"Not really." She gave a tiny shrug. "Over the past few days I have spent a great deal of time with Andre. I have discovered that we have much in common."

Philip should have been delighted. Instead his

brows snapped together. "And what of your protests that you only wished to marry for love?"

"You have made such an opportunity impossible, my lord."

Philip flinched at the bald statement. How could he protest? It was no less than the truth, as unpalatable as it might be. He felt his heart clench, wondering why he was not celebrating his moment of triumph.

Could it be that he did not wish her to wed Andre? Had he come to realize the timid young man and his harpy of a mother were not worthy of Bella? "I did ask if you wished a season," he reminded her stiffly.

Her expression became mocking. "After you have already selected my husband? That seems rather absurd."

"It will give you an opportunity to become more comfortable with the thought of marriage. Besides, you would no doubt enjoy the various entertainments to be found."

Somehow, he expected her to leap at the opportunity to postpone her wedding. Surely, a few days with LeMont could not possibly have made her anxious for marriage? The gentleman might be decent enough, but he was no Byron. Still, the stubborn jut of her chin refused to waver.

"I have no desire for a season, but I will require a trousseau. I presume I shall be allowed to travel to London for a proper dressmaker?"

How could she be thinking of dresses? he wondered with a flare of restless dissatisfaction. "Have you given this proper thought?" he abruptly demanded.

"Me?" She jerkily rose to her feet, her expression

annoyed. "I had no intention to wed. You are the one who arranged this match."

"Yes, but there is no great urgency," he inanely argued.

"I thought you wished the wedding to be held in June?"

"That was before you disappeared. It will be difficult to make the arrangements before the end of the summer. It might even be best if we waited until next spring."

He was attempting to be as generous and understanding as possible. Precisely what she claimed she desired from him. But with her usual perversity, she appeared remarkably annoyed with his concessions.

"I have no desire for a lavish wedding. A simple ceremony will suit both Andre and me. There is no need to wait."

There is every need to wait, Philip seethed. With every passing moment, he was becoming more certain that he had made a mistake in choosing LeMont as her husband. "I will not have my ward married in a shabby fashion."

She threw up her hands in exasperation. "Very well, my lord, but I must still go to London to begin making plans."

He wanted to continue the argument, but he could already hear the sound of guests arriving. He would have to postpone his desire to call off the wedding until a more appropriate moment. "We will go to London at the end of the week."

Fifteen

Sipping his brandy, Philip brooded on his current ill humor. It was absurd. Now that he had returned to London, he should be devoting his attention to the vast stack of invitations littering his foyer, or indulging his senses in the practiced delights of Miss Ravel. Instead, he was attempting to drown his thoughts in this exclusive gentleman's club.

What the devil was wrong with Miss Bella Lowe? For weeks, she had pouted and raved that she had no desire to wed Andre LeMont. Now, as he slowly began to accept that he had acted rashly, she was suddenly determined to marry the jackanapes.

Good lord, the man was not worthy of her. She needed a gentleman who could appreciate her impetuous nature and shrewd intelligence. A gentleman like . . . himself.

A sharp pain jolted through his body as he raised his glass and drained it in one gulp.

Fool. Fool. Fool.

He was Bella's guardian. What sort of guardian longed to seduce his own ward? To make her his wife and fill her with his children? He was beyond reproach.

Leaning forward to pour himself another healthy measure of the fiery spirit, Philip abruptly became aware that someone had halted beside his chair. Turning his head, he regarded the intruder with a fierce scowl. The scowl was only mildly tempered by the realization of who was impinging upon his privacy.

"Good god, Simon," he said. "What the devil are you doing here? I thought you were in the wilds of Devonshire?"

"I was," Simon retorted with a grimace. "And I must warn you that my travels have left me in a foul mood."

"It cannot be any more foul than my own." He waved a slender hand toward the wing chair on the opposite side of the fireplace. "Have a seat."

Simon settled his tall frame into the supple leather and motioned for a hovering servant. "Your best brandy," he commanded. "And plenty of it."

"Yes, my lord." The uniformed man bowed and walked toward a heavy side table. In the blink of an eye, he returned with a crystal-cut decanter and glass.

"Devonshire not all that you wished?" Philip demanded as he watched Simon pour himself a drink and promptly toss it down his throat.

"Devonshire was fine. It was my ill-tempered shrew of a neighbor that was impossible."

Philip's elegantly handsome features tightened. There was an edge to his friend's tone, and a hectic glitter in his eyes that warned him what was troubling him. "A female, I presume?"

Simon poured another measure of brandy. "Claire the bloody cat."

A cat? He was upset over a cat? "Pardon me?"

"Miss Blakewell," Simon muttered in explanation. "An unruly, ungrateful spitfire with the manners of a street urchin."

Ah, so it was a woman, Philip concluded. And a woman much like Bella Lowe, if he did not miss his guess. "Did I not warn you that it was safer to battle Napoleon than to battle the wiles of a cunning female?"

"I will certainly drink to that." Simon emptied his glass. "What of you? How could your mood be foul when you have been surrounded by the comforts of London and the lovely charm of Miss Ravel?"

"Unfortunately, I just returned to London. I was called away."

"Called away to where?"

"Surrey."

"Good God, why?"

Philip's lips thinned. "My ward."

"Ah. I thought she resided at your estate?"

Philip could not halt his sharp laugh. "It is a long, unfortunate tale. Let it just be said that at the moment I would like nothing better than to lock her in a cellar and toss away the key."

Simon lifted his glass with a mocking smile. "Hear. Hear. To deep cellars with thick doors and . . ."

A sudden disruption across the room had Philip turning to discover Huber discretely attempting to turn away the unsteady form of a drunken guest. A flare of disbelief raced through him as he recognized Lord Wickton. With a frown, Philip rose to his feet, and in the same motion as Simon, moved toward their friend.

"Stand aside, Huber," Lord Wickton was demanding in thick tones.

"My lord, please."

"Stand aside or be prepared to defend yourself."

Realizing that Barth was more than a bit bosky, Philip firmly grasped him about the shoulders. "Good God, Wickton, come along."

Too muddled to argue, Barth allowed himself to be led toward the distant corner, not even protesting when Simon pressed him into a seat. "Challmond? Brasleigh?" He attempted to gather his composure. "What the devil are you doing here?"

"Clearly the same thing you have been doing for quite some time," Simon informed him.

Barth shrugged, then gave a smile as his gaze landed upon the decanter beside the chair. "Ah . . . brandy. Just what I need."

"Coffee," Philip corrected as he whisked the spirits out of the reach of the foxed nobleman and handed it to the hovering Huber. "Now why are you not in Kent with your new bride?"

"There is no bride," he snapped.

Philip and Simon exchanged a startled glance.

"I thought the marriage was arranged?" Simon retorted.

"As did I." Barth allowed his head to lay back and closed his eyes. "Unfortunately, the bride has decided that she prefers another. And I must say I do not blame her. He is an absolutely brilliant gentleman without a fault to be discovered. And believe me, I have tried."

"That is rather a bad break, but she is not the only maiden in England. You will soon find another bride," Philip attempted to console him.

"Oh, yes, there are no doubt any number of maidens willing to become the countess of Wickton." Barth opened his eyes, his expression harsh with pain. "A pity I do not bloody well want them."

Philip shivered even as he forced himself to give

another laugh. "Well, are we not a sad trio? What happened to the 'Casanova Club'? Love them and leave them wishing for more?"

"It is all that gypsy's fault," Barth muttered. "Her and her devil's curse."

"Absurd," Simon denied.

"Then you have not tumbled into the stormy seas of love?" Barth challenged.

"Love?" Simon appeared as if he had been struck by lightning, but before he could confess what had caused such a stark expression, a servant halted at his side.

"My lord."

"Yes?" Simon demanded.

"A message has been delivered for you."

"Thank you."

Philip and Barth waited in silence as their friend swiftly read the missive and then abruptly crushed it into a tight ball. "Damnation!"

Philip was instantly concerned. He did not like seeing his friends so obviously at the mercy of their emotions. No more than he enjoyed being a prisoner to his own. "Troubles?"

"It is from Locky."

"Locky?" Barth hiccuped. "Where the devil is he?"

"Devonshire. I have to leave."

"Wait." Philip reached out a hand to halt his impetuous friend. "Is there something that we can do to help?"

"As a matter of fact, you can wish me luck," Simon said in soft tones. "I am off to win the heart of the woman I love."

Philip could only watch Simon stride from the room with a distinct pang in his heart. A pang that might have been envy. At least he was in the position to proclaim his love. Unlike himself.

"The woman he loves?" Barth intruded into his thoughts. "Poor sod. Where is that brandy?"

"I believe you have indulged enough for one evening." Philip returned to his own seat and glanced at his decidedly foxed companion.

"Oh, no, I have not indulged nearly enough."

Philip frowned. "What troubles you?"

"Isa Lawford troubles me," Barth muttered.

Good gads. Another brave member of the Casanova Club ruined by a female, Philip acknowledged.

"I thought you did not wish to wed the chit?" Philip retorted. Certainly Barth had never hidden his dislike at being forced down the aisle.

"I was a bloody fool."

"Then you wish her to be your wife?"

"Yes."

Philip slowly leaned forward. His own life might be in chaos, but there was no reason for Barth to suffer. Not if he could help. "Do you love her?"

"Love?" Barth closed his eyes. "What is that?"

"How do you feel when you are near her?"

"As if my guts are being twisted into a knot. Is that love?"

Philip's expression was mocking. "I certainly hope not."

Barth slowly opened his eyes and banged a fist on the arm of his chair. "But the beastly thing is that I cannot get her out of my mind. I came to London to enjoy my freedom. After all, I have spent a lifetime being smothered by the knowledge that I would have to wed Isa Lawford to save the Wickton family from disgrace. I should be relieved at the thought that she has refused to become my wife."

Philip thought of his own chastisements to be

happy that Bella Lowe was soon to become Mrs. LeMont. What better means of putting her out of his thoughts than to give her to another? Unfortunately, it had served no better purpose than to make him more miserable than ever.

"But you are not relieved?"

"I have never been so bloody miserable in all my life," he confessed. "Isa may no longer be my fiancée, but she refuses to leave me in peace."

It was a complaint all too familiar to Philip. "Do not tell me. She is there every time you close your eyes. You smell her scent in the air, and when you awake in the morning, your arms ache because she is not lying beside you."

"How did you know?" Barth breathed.

Philip struggled to regain his composure. He was supposed to be helping his friend, not bemoaning his own troubles. "What will you do?"

Barth's expression hardened. "Nothing."

"Nothing?"

"I have been informed that a true gentleman should bow out with as much grace as possible."

Philip regarded his friend with stern disapproval. Bow out, indeed. "I have never known you to give up, Wickton. Remember when we were surrounded by those damned Frenchies and our commander wanted to retreat? You pulled out your sword and demanded that we fight our way through."

"I would rather face a regiment of Frenchies than a devious woman. At least I knew what was expected of me."

Philip could not help but agree. "Hear. Hear."

"You were wise not to become entangled in the dangerous lures of a female."

"Oh, yes, I am all that is wise," Philip retorted in mocking tones. "What will you do?"

It took Barth a moment to answer. "I do not know."

"What do you want?" Philip demanded. He waited for his friend to respond, but Barth appeared lost in his dark thoughts. "Barth?"

Barth gave a sharp shake of his head. "What do I want? I want to see Isa smile."

Philip caught his breath. Such simple words, and yet they made his heart twist with an aching sense of loss. He had been fighting Bella for so long, it seemed.

What would he give to see her smile at him?

"Bloody hell." Barth swayed to his feet.

Philip swiftly rose as well. "Where are you going?"

Barth gave a short laugh. "To do the one good thing I may ever do in my miserable, self-indulgent life."

Reaching out to halt his friend, Philip suddenly dropped his hand and allowed Barth to make his way unsteadily out of the room. Although he had always been the one to rush to the rescue of his friends, it was clear that both Simon and Barth would have to solve their problems on their own on this occasion. When it came to matters of the heart, he was the last person to offer advice.

Once again on his own, Philip returned to his seat and poured himself another glass of brandy. In many ways he envied his friends. At least they appeared determined to do something about their feelings.

He wanted to do the same. He wanted to rush to his mother's town house, where he had installed Bella, and command her not to wed Andre. He wanted to tell her . . .

"My lord, excuse me."

Annoyed at once again being interrupted, Philip lifted his head to discover his footman standing beside him with an apologetic expression.

"Yes?"

"You asked me to inform you if anything unusual occurred with Miss Lowe."

Philip's heart slammed to a halt. It had been more impulse than logic that had urged him to keep a careful watch on his ward. "What is it?"

"She has left Lady Claypole's assembly."

"Alone?"

The young man reddened in embarrassment. "She traveled down the street and then halted at a corner and a gentleman entered the carriage."

Blast the unruly brat. "Who?"

"Monsieur LeMont."

"You are certain?" he demanded, even as he realized that it could be no one else. What other gentleman did she know in London?

"Yes, my lord."

"Where did they go?"

"They are at a small posting inn outside of London."

"The devil they are."

In a heartbeat Philip was on his feet. Clearly, the two had realized that he was opposed to their marriage and that in the end he would discover some means of preventing their being together. So they rashly presumed that they could sneak away and perform the deed. Well, not as long as he had a breath in his body. Bella was not marrying Andre. At least not until he told her how he felt.

"Come."

***

The posting inn left much to be desired. Loud, shabby, and reeking of stale food and unwashed bodies, it appeared to cater to those who had nothing more on their minds than to consume as much ale as was possible. Thankfully, Bella had possessed money enough to reserve a private sitting room as well as enough to bribe the innkeeper into ensuring that she was left in peace.

Not that Bella intended to linger for long. Once that she was certain that Andre and Claudette were well on their way to Scotland, she would command the carriage she had hired to take her to Lady Stenhold's friend. She had already sent her own carriage back to Lady Brasleigh's in the hope that they would believe she had left with Andre. She would arrive at her destination empty-handed, but Lady Stenhold had assured her that all would be well.

At least she would be away from Lord Brasleigh, she acknowledged with a flare of pain.

The past week had been nearly unbearable. He had seemed to be constantly underfoot, remaining throughout the day and even for dinner. At every turn, she could see his handsome countenance and smell the lingering scent of his cologne. Even worse, he had all but realized that a marriage between herself and Andre was absurd. She had had to work swiftly to ensure her plan worked.

And—unbelievably—it had.

Within the hour, she would be in her new home, and she could begin to make her own plans for the future. There would be no companions, no guardians, no one at all to interfere.

She was free.

Determinedly attempting to convince herself that she would be happy without Lord Brasleigh, she was distracted by the sound of raised voices in the hall. Then, without warning, the door to the sitting room was thrust open. Her heart froze as the achingly familiar form of Lord Brasleigh entered the room.

"Bella," he growled, his face flushed with anger.

Her eyes widened with shock. How had he found her? she wondered wildly. She had taken such care.

Not that it mattered now, she told herself, attempting to gather her rattled thoughts. For the moment, she had to think of Andre. Her escape might be postponed, but she could at least ensure that the two lovers were allowed to wed. That meant distracting this intimidating gentleman until they were too far for capture.

"My lord."

His silver eyes flashed. "Where is he?"

"He?" She attempted to appear innocent.

Lord Brasleigh was not deceived for a moment. "Do not play me the fool. Where is LeMont?"

"I haven't the slightest notion."

He moved forward to tower over her seated form. "My groom watched LeMont enter your carriage, so there is little point in lying."

So that was how he knew where she was, Bella seethed. The rat. "You were having me followed?"

"Of course."

"How dare you?"

"Obviously, you are not to be trusted," he retorted without remorse.

His arrogance was beyond belief.

"You are the one not be trusted, my lord," she informed him in angry tones. "I am a young lady, not a common criminal to be spied upon and followed in such a fashion."

"Since you have yet to act the role of a young

lady, I have little recourse but to treat you as a willful chit."

"You, sir, are an insufferable boor," she informed him, furious with the aching pain in the center of her heart. "Please go away."

"I have every intention of going and taking you with me," he threatened. "But first I intend to beat some sense into that young cur."

Bella's protective instincts rose to the fore. It was a lucky that thing Andre was not there; he probably would have fainted at the sight of the furious lord. Bella, however, was made of sterner stuff. "You are to leave Andre alone. If you wish to vent your ill humor onto someone, you can do so to me."

His expression hardened. "You would protect a gentleman who brings you to this godforsaken inn and exposes you to the worse sort of scandal?"

"I came with Andre freely. Indeed, it was my idea."

An odd flicker of distress darkened his silver eyes as his hands clenched into fists. "Do you have no shame?"

"I do not understand why you are so angry," she retorted. "You are the one who wished me to be with Andre."

"Not in this manner."

He was impossible, she decided, thoroughly and utterly impossible. "What a hypocrite you are," she charged.

"No, I am merely beginning to suspect that I made a poor choice in LeMont."

"He is a fine gentleman."

"He is not for you," Lord Brasleigh rasped.

Bella arched her brows. "No?"

"No." There was a throbbing silence. "I am."

Bella nearly tumbled off the sofa in shock. Was

he implying that he . . . No, it was impossible. She had to have misunderstood. "What did you say?"

"Dash it all," he muttered, tossing aside his hat and gloves. "I love you."

Numb with disbelief, she gave a slow shake of her head. This was not at all the arrogant, domineering bully she knew. He suddenly appeared as awkward and uncertain as a schoolboy. There had to be something wrong. "You do not know what you are saying."

"Oh, no?" With jerky movements he lowered himself beside her and grasped her cold fingers in a tight grip. "I know precisely what I am saying. At last."

"But . . . You treat me as a child."

His expression became rueful. "It was the only means of not sweeping you off your feet and into my bed."

Bella felt as if she had plunged into some crazy dream. For too long she had refused to allow herself to hope that things could be different between her and Lord Brasleigh. After all, such thoughts would only lead to further pain. Now she found herself unable to accept that he could actually be saying the words she had longed to hear.

"My lord . . ."

"Philip," he interrupted softly. "My name is Philip."

"You are simply attempting to trick me into going home with you."

His silver eyes darkened to smoke. "Not this time, Bella. No lies, no deceit. I love you. I think that I have loved you from the moment I arrived at Mayfield."

Bella gave a rather hysterical laugh. "That is remarkably difficult to believe."

He possessed the grace to blush. "I will admit that I was angry when you disappeared and I was determined to teach you a lesson. In my arrogance, I presumed it would be a simple matter to frighten you into marriage and then return to my life in London."

"I am well aware of your despicable plot," she reminded him.

His hand reached up to push back a renegade curl. "You had plots of your own, if you will recall, my dear."

This time it was Bella's turn to blush. "Only out of desperation. You deserved much worse."

"Perhaps." That distracting finger moved across her cheek, then softly outlined her trembling lips. "I was a reprehensible guardian, but I intend to be the very best of husbands."

Husband. Bella gave an audible gasp. "You wish to marry me?"

His expression became uncommonly somber. "Only if it is what you wish. I have learned my lesson, Bella. From now on, I will consider only your happiness. If you wish to return to your home, I will ensure that it is properly repaired and you are given a full staff."

A slow, nearly overwhelming surge of happiness began to flood through her body. "Do you mean that?"

"Yes," he said simply.

Abruptly, her lingering fears fled, and a luminous glow of happiness shimmered in her dark eyes. "What if I do not wish to leave?"

He gave a low groan of relief and tugged her against his hard frame. "Then I will make you my wife and never let you go."

Bella had never dared dream that she could feel

such happiness. All thoughts of flight were banished from her mind. She was precisely where she wished to be. "Oh, Philip, I do love you."

"And you will marry me?" he demanded.

"Yes."

With obvious reluctance, he slowly pulled back. "What of LeMont?"

She flashed him a triumphant smile. "Andre left before you arrived. He is eloping with the woman he loves."

Lord Brasleigh was clearly stunned. "Then why are you here?"

"I wanted you to believe that I had left with Andre so that you would not search for me in London."

"Brat," he growled at her cunning, even as he was slowly lowering his head. "I see I shall never be allowed to let you out of my sight."

"Is that a promise?" she teased, her lips already parting in anticipation.

His mouth tenderly brushed her own. "One I intend to keep for an eternity."

Epilogue

The first day of June, Philip entered the London gambling establishment with his required thousand pounds and a single red rose. He ignored the curious glances and even waves of greeting as he strode toward the back corner. He had not wanted to leave Bella. Gads, he never wanted to leave Bella, he acknowledged with a wry grin. If he had thought marriage might ease the burning desire to be at her side, to hold her in his arms, he had been gloriously mistaken.

If anything, the past weeks had only deepened his fascination with the bewitching creature. But the promise to his friends had led him to the strictly male club.

Now, he hurried to conduct his business so he could return to his wife. Approaching the three chairs pulled toward a bay window, a wide smile split his face as Barth rose to his feet. A decidedly more composed Barth than the one he had encountered on his previous trip to London.

"By gads, Philip, it is good to see you."

Philip clasped his hand onto his friend's shoulder. "Hello, Barth."

A pair of mischievous hazel eyes twinkled with

delight as he pointedly glanced at the packet and rose in Philip's hand. "It appears that I am not the only one to have fallen victim to the gypsy's blessing. I must say that I would have wagered you would be the winner. What occurred?"

Philip smiled. "In truth, I haven't the slightest notion. One day I was a perfectly reasonable gentleman, and the next I was as looby as any poor soul in Bedlam. And even worse, I have never been happier in my life."

"Who would have suspected a month ago that we would actually be pleased to lose our wager?"

Philip chuckled, thinking of his blind arrogance. "Not I."

Barth tugged his ear in a familiar manner. "So who is the lucky maiden?"

"My ward, as a matter of fact. And yourself?"

"Miss Lawford."

Philip blinked in surprise. "I thought she loved another?"

"Quite inexplicably, she has decided that she loves me instead."

"And you intend to wed?"

A glow settled on the boyishly handsome countenance. "As soon as she'll have me."

Philip gave his friend another pat, well aware that they were both grinning like daft fools.

"A pity we did not think to order a bottle. We could have raised a toast."

"It is fortunate that I am always prepared for any emergency," a familiar voice suddenly announced.

Philip whirled about to discover Simon, along with a servant who discretely handed Barth and Philip a glass of brandy before fading back into the crowd.

Philip noted the glass already in Simon's slender hand. "Have you come to claim the wager?"

The familiar twinkle was present in Simon's eyes as he pulled his other hand from behind his back to reveal a packet and red rose. "I have come to offer my forfeit," he confessed. "And to offer a toast."

Barth gave a sudden laugh, raising his glass. "To a gypsy's blessing."

Simon lifted his glass. "To true love."

"To three extraordinary ladies," Philip offered. They readily took a deep drink, then glanced toward the table. "What shall we do with the money?"

"There is an orphanage being opened in Wiltshire," Simon retorted. "We could donate the money in the name of the Casanova Club."

Barth instantly agreed. "Hear. Hear."

Philip slowly nodded his head. "A fitting end to the Casanova Club."

ABOUT THE AUTHOR

Debbie Raleigh lives with her family in Missouri. She is currently working on a new Regency romance trilogy, this one focusing on three sisters. Look for THE CHRISTMAS WISH coming in November 2001. Debbie loves to hear from readers, and you may write to her c/o Zebra Books. Please include a self-addressed stamped envelope if you wish a response.

Merlin's Legacy

A Series From
Quinn Taylor Evans